THE ILLUSTRATED STORY-TELLER.

THE

CORSICAN BROTHERS.

"THINK OF GOD, MY SON."

LONDON: W. S. JOHNSON, 60, ST. MARTIN'S LANE, CHARING CROSS.

TO BE HAD OF ALL BOOKSELLERS.

THE

CORSICAN BROTHERS.

"There are more assassinations take place among us, than among any other people: but never will you find an ignoble cause or motive for these crimes. We have, it is true, a great many murderers, but not one thief. * * * * Why send powder to a rogue who will use it only for criminal purposes? Owing to the deplorable weakness which the whole people here seem to have in regard to bandits, it will be some time before they disappear from Corsica. * * * * * And what has the bandit done,—for what crime is he forced into the mountains.—Brandolaccio has committed no crime; he killed Giovano Opizzo, who assassinated his father whilst he served in the army."—PROSPER MERIMEE, *Colomba.*

PART I.

CHAPTER I.

IT was early in the month of March, 1841, that I undertook a voyage to Corsica. Now a voyage to Corsica is one of the most pleasant and picturesque in the world. Embarking at Toulon, in twenty hours you reach Ajaccio; in twenty-four you reach Bastia. Your first care, on landing, is to buy or hire a horse; if the latter, you will have to pay five francs a day for its hire: if you buy a horse, you must put down one hundred and fifty francs. Do not sneer at the smallness of the price: for this horse, whether bought or hired, like the famous horse of Gascon, which leaped from the Pont Neuf into the Seine, will do feats far outstripping those of Prospero or Nautilus; those equine heroes of the racecourses at Chantilly and the Champ de Mars. He will take you over roads where Balmat* himself would have put iron cramps on his shoes; and he will cross bridges over which Auriol† would not have hesitated to ask for a balancing pole.

As for the traveller, he has but to shut his eyes, and let his animal go as he pleases: there is no danger, if he does not look at his road.

With this horse, you can reckon on doing your fifteen leagues a day without stopping to eat or to drink. But, from time to time, whilst you stop—perhaps to inspect some old castle built by some feudal lord, the hero of many a fondly cherished tradition, or perhaps to take a sketch of some old tower built by the Genoese—your horse will crop a tuft of grass, make a lunch off the bark of some tree, or lick the moss from a rock; he is satisfied and refreshed.

* Balmat, a famous guide for travellers across the Alps.—*Trans.*

† Auriol, one of the most celebrated posturists and mountebanks of the day.—*Trans.*

With regard to your night's lodging, nothing can be more inartificial; the traveller arrives in some village, goes down the long single street which it contains, and having made choice of the house which best suits him, knocks at the door. The next moment, the master or the mistress of the house is at the threshold, you are invited to walk inside; you are offered a share of the supper, and his own bed, if there is but one, is at your service. In the morning, he escorts you to the door, and thanks you gratefully for the preference you have given to him over his neighbours; for the matter of compensation or payment, there is no question: you could not give a greater insult to your host than to broach a word respecting such a subject. If, however, the traveller has been waited upon by a young girl, he may venture to offer a gay pattern silk kerchief, with which she will make a very picturesque head-dress at the next fair of Calvi or Corte. If a male domestic serves, he will willingly accept a gift of a new dagger or rather dagger-knife, with which he might with equal ease and equal sang froid cut his own dinner or his enemy's throat.

One thing, it may be as well to mention: the domestics, if any, are very often the children of some other proprietor, less opulent than their own master, and who give their services in exchange for food, lodging, and a piastre or two per month. Nor are these masters, having for servants their grand nephews, or cousins, or some other relative up to the fifth or sixth degree of consanguinity, a whit the less better served. Corsica is a French department: but the Corsican is still a great remove from being a Frenchman in mind or manners.

As for thieves, no one ever heard talk of such a thing; but of bandits they have a superabundance: but we must not confound one class with the other. You may go without fear from Ajaccio to Bastia, your bags stuffed with gold hanging at your saddle-bow—you may, indeed, go through the length and breadth of the whole island without running the shadow of risk of losing a sous: but don't venture from Occano to Levaco, if you have an enemy who has declared *la vendetta,* or vengeance, against you; I would not answer for your safe conduct for even two short leagues.

To resume: I was in Corsica at the beginning of March, and alone, for my companion Jadin had remained in Rome. I had sailed from the Isle of Elba, and disembarking at Bastia, I forthwith proceeded to buy a horse, at the price I have before mentioned. I had visited Corte and Ajaccio, and my next point of observation was the province of Sartène. On this particular day, I was travelling from Sartène to Sullacaro. It was but a short stage: but owing to the detour which we were obliged to make round the advanced counterforts of the great chain of mountains, which form, as it were, the backbone of the island, and which required some activity to traverse, it brought our day's travel to about a dozen leagues. I had taken a guide for fear of losing my way among the hills. At five o'clock we reached the summit of the hill which towers above Olmeto and Sullacaro.

"Where would your lordship wish to lodge?" asked the guide.

I cast my eyes upon the village, and gave a glance through its streets, which presented to my view indications of being all but deserted: a female might be seen at rare intervals.

As, by virtue of the established laws of hospitality, to which I have already alluded, I was at liberty to make my choice of any one of the hundred or so of houses of which the village was composed, I looked out very keenly for the domicile which appeared to me to give the best chances of comfort; and at last, I pointed out a square built house, constructed in the style of a fortress, with battlemented windows and portcullised doors. It was the first specimen I had seen of those domestic fortifications; but I should also add that the province of Sartène is the classic land of *la vendetta.*

"Good," said my guide, following with his eyes the indication of my hand, "that is the house of Madame Savilia de Franchi. Your lordship has not made a bad choice; and that you will perceive when you come to the proof."

I should here remark that in this, the eighty-sixth department of France, Italian is invariably spoken.

"But," objected I, "would it be quite convenient to demand hospitality from a lady? for, if I understood you, you said the house belonged to a lady."

"Doubtless," replied he, with an air of astonishment, "but what inconvenience can your lordship fancy from that circumstance?"

"Why, if the lady is young," I replied, actuated by a feeling of propriety, or perhaps, to tell the truth, from the self-opinion natural to a Parisian, "if the lady is young, a night passed by me under her roof might compromise her."

"Compromise her?" repeated the guide, in a state of bewilderment, and evidently vainly searching his brains for a meaning to the word I had rashly Italianized, with that *à plomb* which ordinarily characterises a Frenchman, when he ventures to speak in a foreign language.

"Well—well! Doubtless the lady is a widow?" asked I, in an impatient tone.

"Yes, Excellency."

"Very good—now, would she admit a young man into her home?" In 1844, I had numbered thirty-six summers, and I called myself still a young man.

"Would she admit a young man?" slowly repeated the guide, and then quickly adding, "Well! what has she to fear, whether you are young or old?"

I saw plainly that it was useless to continue this mode of interrogation. "How old is Madame Savilia?" I asked.

"About forty."

"Ah!" answered I, more in response to my own thoughts than aloud, "then of course she has children?"

"Two sons—two fine young men."

"Shall I see them?"

"You will see one of them: he lives at home."

"And where is the other?"

"In Paris."

"And how old are they?"

"Twenty-one."

"What—both of them?"

"Yes; they are twin brothers."

"And for what profession are they destined?"

"The one in Paris will be brought up to the law."

"And the other?"

"Will be a Corsican."

"Ah! ah!" for I could not help laughing at the characteristic reply, uttered, as it was, in a tone inimitable for simplicity. "Very well: let us go to the house of Madame Savilia de Franchi." So saying, we resumed our journey, and ten minutes' walk brought us into the village. As we passed along its streets, I noticed one feature in the architecture of the houses which I could not perceive from the distant hills around. All the houses were fortified, similar to that of Madame Savilia's—not with battlements and portcullises, for the poverty of the owners of most forbade those luxuries; but the lower windows of the houses were all fortified strongly with stout planks, leaving loopholes for the discharge of musketry. The other windows were fortified in like manner by red bricks. On asking my guide the term given to those loopholes, he answered by telling me they were called arrow-holes; a reply which fully convinced me that the Corsican *vendetta* had a greater antiquity than the invention of firearms. The farther we advanced into the village, the more profoundly desolate and melancholy grew its aspect. I remarked too, that many of the houses appeared to have sustained a recent siege or assault, for the walls bore many a mark and indentation from musket balls. Occasionally, while gazing at the loopholed windows, we might catch a glance of some curious eye looking at us as we passed up the solitary street: but from that glance it was impossible to say whether the eyes belonged to a man or a woman.

"At a turn in the corridor, I found myself face to face with a lady of very tall stature dressed in black."—*Page 5.*

We stopped at the house which I had pointed out to my guide, and which was, in fact, the most imposing mansion in the place. I was rather surprised at finding, on coming close to the edifice, that fortified as the house was in appearance, by the battlements and portcullises I had observed at some distance, it was not so in reality; the windows were not protected by planks, bricks, or loopholes, but exhibited the simple squares of glass, with wooden shutters to protect them at night. Certainly these window-shutters presented features which, to a practised eye, showed unmistakeable marks of bullet-holes. But these were not of recent date, and bore the appearance of at least a dozen years elapsing since they were made.

My guide had scarcely knocked ere the door was opened, not cautiously or hesitatingly, or suspiciously, but flung widely open, and, with an air of grandeur, a valet appeared. I said a valet—I was wrong, I should have said a man; the livery makes the valet; and the individual who opened the door to us was clothed in a simple dress of velvet, with breeches of the same material, and his legs encased in untanned leather gaiters. Round his waist he wore a variegated silk sash, from which peeped out the handle of a murderous-looking Spanish dagger.

"My friend," said I to him, "is it improper for me, a stranger, to come here for the purpose of claiming the hospitality of your mistress?"

"Certainly not, Excellence," said he, "the

"I felt an irresistible wish to make an inventory o my abode and its contents."—*Page 6.*

stranger honors the home at which it is his pleasure to stop. Maria," said he, turning round and speaking to a female servant who was behind him, "inform Madame Savilia that a French traveller seeks hospitality."

Almost at the same moment, a step-ladder of eight or nine rounds was lowered from the gate above, and the valet descended and took the bridle of my horse. I dismounted.

"Your Excellence has no occasion to trouble yourself: all your baggage shall be brought into your room."

I profited by this kind invitation to my laziness—by-the-way, one of the most agreeable things you can do for a weary traveller.

CHAPTER II.

WITH a light step, I ascended the ladder above-mentioned, and found myself in the interior of the house. At a turn in the corridor, I found myself face to face with a lady of very tall stature, dressed in black. I could instantly divine that this lady, apparently of thirty-eight or forty years of age, though still handsome, was the mistress of the house, and I accordingly stopped.

"Madame," said I, bowing, "you may, perhaps, think me very indiscreet; but the custom of your country will perhaps be my best excuse, together with the invitation of your authorised servant."

"You are welcomed by the mother, and you

will be by her son whenever he comes in. From this moment, monsieur, the house is your own : use it, then, as if it was yours."

"I would trespass on your kindness for one night only, madame. At day-break, to-morrow morning, I shall take my leave."

"You are at liberty to stay as long or as short as you please, monsieur. Nevertheless, I hope that you will change your mind, and that we shall be honoured by your presence as our guest for some time."

I bowed low a second time.

"Maria," continued Madame Franchi, and addressing the servant girl, "conduct the gentleman to Louis's chamber. Light a fire in his room immediately, and carry him hot water. Excuse me, sir," turning to me, whilst the servant went to perform her instructions, "I know the first wants of a traveller are fire and water. You will follow the girl, sir, and don't forget to ask for whatever you may require. In an hour's time supper will be on the table, by which time my son will be here, and will have the honour of requesting your presence at table."

"You will excuse my travelling costume, madame ?"

"On this condition, sir, that you will, on your side, excuse the rusticity of your reception."

The servant ascended the staircase, and I, bowing to the lady a third time, followed.

The room was on the first floor, and looked out from the back of the house : its windows opened upon a large and pretty garden, thickly planted with myrtles and rose-laurels, and was crossed in all directions by a little rivulet which finally ran into the Tavaro. At the end of the garden, the view was bounded by a thick hedge of fir trees, so closely growing that it served almost as a boundary wall. As is usual in the rooms of Italian houses, the walls were lime-washed, ornamented here and there by some fresco landscapes.

I felt an irresistible wish, whilst Maria was occupied in lighting the fire and preparing the water, to make an inventory of my abode and its contents, and to form, by the aid of the furniture and arrangements, an idea as to the character and disposition of its former occupant. I began immediately to execute my project by making a pivot of my left heel, and slowly passing in review the various articles of furniture which were in the room. The furniture was all modern, in fact—taking into consideration that this portion of the island was quite young in its civilization— might be said to manifest a luxury very rarely to be seen. It comprised an iron bedstead, on which were three mattresses and a pillow, also a sofa, four arm-chairs, six other chairs, and a goodly assortment of books ranged on a double-shelfed bookcase, and a bureau, and the whole was of the finest grained mahogany, and evidently from the shop of the first cabinet-maker in Ajaccio. The sofa and chairs were covered with flowered Indian cotton prints, and moreen curtains hung around the two windows, and enveloped the bed. I had got thus far in my catalogue, when the exit of Maria enabled me to pursue my investigations to a more minute extent. I opened the bookcase, and I found a collection of all our greatest poets, Corneille, Racine, Molière, La Fontaine, Rousard,

Victor Hugo, and Lamartine ; of moralists there were Montaigne, Pascal, and La Bruyère : in history, Mézery, Châteaubriand, and Augustin Thiery. In science—Cuvier, Beudant, Elie de Beaumont ; and lastly, a few volumes of novels, amongst which I found with no small amount of self-pride, my "Impressions of Travels." The keys were on the bureau : I opened one of the drawers. I there found some fragments of a History of Corsica ; a work upon the means necessary to abolish the custom of *la vendetta* ; some French verses ; Italian sonnets—all in manuscript. I had now as much ground-work to build upon as I wished ; and I needed no further research to enable me to draw my imaginary portrait of the characteristics and opinions of M. Louis Franchi. He was, in short, a mild, studious young man, and a partizan of the reform school. I could well understand, then, that he had gone to Paris to qualify himself as an advocate : he had, no doubt, the intention to carry out his project of effecting the civilization of his country by this means.

I made these reflections whilst I was dressing. My appearance, as I had hinted to Madame Franchi, though wanting nothing in respect of the picturesque, needed a certain amount of indulgence in the dining-room. It was composed of a velvet jacket, opened at the seams of the sleeves, in order to give free ingress to the air during the sultry hours of my travelling—and, whilst this gave to it the appearance of a Spanish slashed doublet, it revealed a shirt of striped silk : pantaloons of the same material : from the knee to the foot was embraced by Spanish gaiters, fastened at the sides with colored silk ; a felt hat, of easy temper, taking any shape you pleased to make it, but more particularly useful in the form of a Spanish sombrero.

I had just finished my toilet, as above given, —and which costume I would especially recommend to travellers as one of the most useful I know of—when the door opened, and the same individual who had at first introduced me to the house, appeared : he announced to me that his young master, M. Lucien de Franchi, had just arrived, and sent to beg the honour of welcoming me, as soon as it might be convenient. Of course I replied that all the honor would be conferred on myself. A moment after his departure, I heard the quick step of one approaching my room, and I stood in the presence of my host.

CHAPTER III.

My host was, as my guide correctly informed me, a young man, of about twenty-one ; with black hair and eyes, features embrowned with the sun, short in stature, but with well-formed limbs. In his haste to present his compliments to me, he had not waited to change his riding costume : his coat was of green cloth, to which the sash round his waist gave a half military feature : pantaloons of grey cloth, mounted with Russian leather, boots and spurs : a cap somewhat similar to those worn by our African chasseurs completed his costume. From the one side of his girdle hung a bottle-gourd, and in the other a pistol was stuck. Besides the last, in his hands he carried an English carbine. Notwithstanding his youth, his upper lip was shaded by a light moustache: altogether there was a striking air of independence and resolution about him. He looked a man risen above his fellows by actual struggle: one accustomed to live in the midst of danger without fear, but at the same time without scorning it; grave in his manners from the solitude of his life; calm, because of the knowledge of his strength. With one glance of his eye he saw everything; my habits, my travelling baggage, my arms—the clothes I had thrown off—those which I wore: indeed that one rapid glance of his eye informed me that he was a man who had often found his life to depend on the strength and comprehension of his sight.

"You will excuse me if I disturb you, monsieur," said he to me, "but I have come with a good intent—to see if you were in need of anything. It is always with a sort of trepidation that we see you gentlemen from the Continent come to our homes—for you know we Corsicans are as yet only half-civilized—and, as I say, it is not without trembling that we exercise, side by side with a Frenchman, those old rites of hospitality which, very shortly, will be the only tradition remaining to us from our fathers."

"And you are wrong to have any fear on the subject, monsieur," responded I; "it would be a difficult task to anticipate the wants of a traveller better than has Madame de Franchi. Besides," continued I, throwing in my turn a rapid glance at the furniture of the apartment, "it is not here that I could complain of that pretended barbarism which you have so good-humouredly alluded to: indeed, if it was not for the beautiful country view from the windows, I might easily believe myself to be in a room in the Chaussée d'Antin."

"Yes," replied the young man, "it was a fancy of my poor brother Louis: he loved to live like a Frenchman; but I much doubt, if on his return from Paris, this poor parody of civilization that he has left behind him will have the same charms for him it had before his departure."

"Has your brother been absent from Corsica any time?" asked I of my young friend.

"The last six months."

"Do you expect him home shortly?"

"Not for three or four years."

"It is a long absence for two brothers, who, I dare say, have never before been separated."

"Yes, and more than all, for two brothers who love each other as we do."

"In all probability he will pay you a visit before finishing his studies?"

"Very likely: at all events he has promised he will do so."

"But, either way, there is nothing to hinder you from going to see him?"

"I shall never quit Corsica!"

He said this in an accent which showed that he was imbued with that intense love of country which leads its owner to despise every other place in the universe. I smiled.

"I dare say it appears strange to you," continued he, echoing my smile; "that we should have no wish to leave a miserable country like ours. But you know nothing of it. I am a part of the produce of the island, as much as its green oaks and its laurel roses; this island gives me an atmosphere loaded with the perfume of the sea, and the health-giving breeze of the mountain; it gives torrents to cross, rocks to climb, forests to explore; it gives me space—it gives me liberty. If I were to be transported into a city, it seems to me that I should immediately fade and die."

"But how can you account for such a great moral difference existing between you and your brother?"

"And with such an exact physical resemblance, you would have added, if you had ever seen both."

"Do you resemble each other very much then?"

"So much, that when we were children, our parents were forced to put a distinguishing mark on our clothes, in order to know the one from the other."

"And in size?"

"Exactly the same: a slight difference in our complexion, produced by the dissimilarity of our pursuits, is the only visible mark of distinction. Always shut up in his room, intent on his books and his drawings, my brother is fair; while I on the contrary, always in the open air, ever scouring the mountains or the plain—I am, as you see, brown."

"I hope," said I to him, "that you will enable me to judge for myself as to your likeness to each other, by giving me a commission to visit M. Louis de Franchi."

"Certainly; and with the greatest pleasure, if you will have the kindness so to do. But, pardon me, I see that you have the advantage of myself with regard to your dress, and in a quarter of an hour's time supper will be on the table."

"I hope it's not on my account that you are troubling yourself to change your dress."

"And if it were so, after the example you have yourself given, you could scarce say a word on the subject. At all events, being now in my riding costume, it will be necessary for me to change it for the dress of a mountaineer. Besides, after supper I have to go where my boots and spurs would be rather in the way."

"Are you going out after supper?" I asked.

"Yes," he replied, "I have an appointment." I smiled.

"Ah—it is not an appointment of the sort that you are thinking of: it is an affair of business."

"You must think me possessed of a good stock of assurance, to believe that I have a right to your confidence."

"Why so? we should always so live as to be able to speak publicly of our actions. But I never had a lover: never shall. If my brother marries and has children, it is very probable that I shall never marry at all. If, on the contrary, he does not take a wife, it will in that case be necessary that I should do so, but it will be only for the sake of preventing the extinction of our family. I have told you," added he, laughing, "that I am a real barbarian—in fact, I was born a century too late. But here I am chattering like a magpie; and at supper-time I shall not be ready."

JARDIN

"I really thought, at a first glance, that I was introduced into a veritable arsenal."—Page 8.

"But we can continue our conversation," said I. "Is not that your chamber opposite? leave the door ajar, and we can talk whilst we dress."

"Better than that even, if you come into my room. I will dress in the inner apartment: it appears to me, from the glance you threw around, you are an amateur of weapons of warfare : look at those in my room: there are some among them, which, historically speaking, are of great value.

CHAPTER IV.

The invitation given me by my host agreed too well with my inclination to compare the rooms of the two brothers, for me to hesitate in accepting it, and I followed him. Opening the door of his apartment, he passed into it before me, to lead the way. I really thought, at a first glance, that I was introduced into a veritable arsenal. All the furniture in the room was of the fifteenth and sixteenth centuries: the bed, carved elaborately from the floor to the canopy, which was sustained by huge twisted columns, was curtained in green gold-flowered damask : the curtains of the windows were of the same material, the walls of the apartment were covered with Spanish leather ; and at frequent intervals, the furniture served as brackets for ancient and modern weapons.

There was no mistaking the predilections of the owner of the room: he was evidently as pugnacious

JARDIN

"'I learnt yesterday that my first-born had been killed in the defence of his country; and I have travelled twenty leagues
to bring my second to its succour."—*Page* 10.

and bellicose as his brother was peaceful and studious.

"Now look about you," said he to me, as he passed into his closet. "You will find yourself in the midst of the evidences of three ages. By-the-by, I am going to put on my mountaineer costume, as immediately after supper I have to go out."

"And how am I to find among all these swords, arquebuses, and poignards, those historical vestiges of which you have spoken?"

"There are three of them in particular. Look at the head of my bed, and you will find a poignard hanging from a large shell, the handle forming a signet.

"I have it. Well?"

"That is the dagger of Sampiero."

"Of the famous Sampiero, the assassin of Vanina?"

"Not the assassin: the murderer."

"It appears to me the terms are synonymous."

"In every other place, perhaps; but not in Corsica."

"And this is an authenticated relic?"

"Inspect it, and you will find Sampiero's arms engraven on it; you will not see the lily of France on it, because, as you know, he was not authorized to carry the fleur-de-lis on his escutcheon until after the siege of Perpignan."

"I was really ignorant of that fact. And how came this poignard into your possession?"

"Oh, it has been in our family for the last three hundred years. It was the gift of Sampiero himself, to one Napoleon de Franchi."

"Do you know the circumstances attending the gift?"

"Yes. Sampiero and my great grandfather had the misfortune to fall into an ambuscade formed by the Genoese; and in the encounter, during which they fought with desperation, Sampiero's helmet fell from his head, and a mounted Genoese was about to give him a *coup de grace* with his mace, when my respected ancestor plunged his dagger into a part of the cavalier's body which was unprotected by his armour: the cavalier, feeling himself wounded, put spurs to his horse, and took to flight, carrying with him the poignard of his adversary, for the blow had been given with such goodwill that my ancestor could not withdraw his weapon. As the dagger was a favorite weapon with my grandfather, and he regretted its loss, Sampiero gave him his own in compensation: Napoleon took care not to lose this, for it was of the finest Spanish steel, as you may see, and will easily pierce through two five-franc pieces laid one on the other."

"May I make trial of it?"

"Do so."

Putting two five-franc pieces on the mantel-piece, I struck with the poignard a quick but vigorous blow on them. Lucien had spoken truly: for when I lifted the poignard, the two five-franc pieces came with it, pierced through with its point."

"Proceed—proceed," said I, "there is no doubt of its being Sampiero's poignard. But one thing surprises me, and that is, why he should have used the cord to his wife when he had such an inimitable weapon as this."

"He had it not at that period: since he had parted with it to my great grandfather."

"Right—right."

"Sampiero was upwards of sixty years of age when he came from Constantinople to Aix, for the express purpose of giving this grand lesson to the world—that it is not the province of females to intermeddle with state affairs."

I bowed in token of acquiescence; and replaced the poignard.

"And now," said I to Lucien, who had by this time finished his toilet, "I have replaced Sampiero's poignard on its nail: let us pass on to the others."

"You perceive those two portraits hanging side by side?"

"Yes, Paoli and Napoleon."

"Good; well near Paoli's portrait hangs a sword."

"Certainly."

"Well, that sword was his."

"The sword of Paoli. And is this equally authenticated?"

"At least, this was also given by its owner—not to one of my great grandfathers, but one of my great grandmothers."

"To one of your grandmothers?"

"Yes. But perhaps you have heard of this lady, who, during the War of Independence, came one day to the castle of Sullacaro, accompanied by a young man."

"No; but pray recount the story."

"It is not a very long one."

"So much the worse."

"We have not much leisure for a long chat."

"I am listening."

"Well, this lady and the young man presented themselves before the gates of the castle, and demanded to speak with Paoli; but as Paoli was at that moment busily engaged in writing, they were refused admittance; and as the lady insisted on being allowed to enter, the two sentinels proceeded to eject her by force. Meanwhile the disturbance had been heard by Paoli, who opening his study door, demanded to know what had occasioned it.

"'It is I who am the cause,' said the lady, 'and I wish to have speech with you.'

"'What have you to say to me?'

"'I have come to tell you that I have two sons. I learnt yesterday that my first-born had been killed in the defence of his country: and I have travelled twenty leagues to bring my second to its succour.'"

"It is a Spartan tale that you are relating."

"There is something of resemblance."

"Who was this lady?"

"She was my grandmother. Paoli unbuckled his sword and gave it into her hand."

"I rather like this mode of apologising to a lady."

"She was worthy of it, was she not?"

"And now, what of this sabre?"

"It is that which Bonaparte wore at the Battle of the Pyramids."

"And doubtless came into the possession of your family in as remarkable a manner as the poignard and sword?"

"Not a doubt of it. After that battle, Bonaparte gave orders to my grandfather, then an officer in the Guides, to charge, with one hundred and fifty men, a knot of Mamelukes which still held their ground around their chief, who had been wounded. My grandfather followed out his instructions, dispersed the Mamelukes, and brought the wounded chief to the First Consul. But, when he tried to sheathe his sword, he found that it was so hacked and hewed by the Damascus blades of his opponents, that no efforts could make it enter the sheath. So, as the sword and sheath were utterly useless for service, my grandfather threw them aside. Bonaparte observing this, gave him that sabre of his own."

"But," said I, "were I in your place, I should place a much higher value on the battered sabre of my ancestor, all hacked and notched as it had been, than on that of the general-in-chief, however sound and well-tempered it might be."

"Look immediately opposite, and you will find it. The Consul took it, caused the diamond you see to be inlaid in its hilt, and sent it to our family as a heirloom, with an inscription on it, which you may read by looking at the blade."

In reality, between the two windows, half in half out of its sheath, hung the disfigured and maimed sabre, with this inscription engraved on it, "BATTLE OF THE PYRAMIDS, 21 JULY, 1798." Just at this moment, the same serving-man who had first introduced me to the mansion, and who had announced to me the arrival of his young master, appeared at the threshold.

"Excellency!" said he, addressing himself to Lucien, "Madame de Franchi wishes to inform you that supper is served."

"Very well, Griffo," answered the young man:

"tell my mother that we are about to come down."

At the same time he came out of his dressing-room, accoutred, as I have said, like a mountaineer —namely, a round velvet jacket, breeches, and gaiters : of his former costume, he retained only the cartouche-box which was fastened to his sash.

He found me engaged in looking at two carbines, suspended opposite each other, each of them having engraven on the butt end : "21 SEPTEMBER, 1819—ONE O'CLOCK IN THE MORNING."

"These carbines," said I, "are they also historically renowned."

"Yes," replied he, "at all events, as far as our family is concerned. One of them was my father's."

He stopped.

"And whose the other ?" inquired I.

"The other," repeated he, laughing, "the other is my mother's. But let us get down : you know they are waiting for us."

And going first to lead the way, he made a sign for me to follow.

CHAPTER V.

I MUST confess that my whole thoughts, whilst descending to the supper room, were concentrated on the last words of Lucien to me : "The other is my mother's carbine ;" and this made me look at Madame de Franchi, on my entrance, with more of scrutiny and curiosity than I should otherwise have ventured at a first interview.

Her son, on his entering the supper-room, took his mother's hand, and saluted it with the deepest homage and respect, which the lady received with the dignity of a queen.

"Pardon me, my mother," said Lucien : "I fear I have kept you waiting."

"In that case," said I, "the fault is entirely mine. Monsieur Lucien has been speaking to me of, and shewing me some rare curiosities, and I have delayed him by my endless questionings."

"You need not apologise, for I have only this moment entered the room. But," continued the lady, addressing her son, "I was anxious to see you, to ask news respecting Louis."

"Has any affliction befallen your son ?" asked I, of Madame de Franchi.

"Lucien fears as much," said she.

"You have then received a letter from your brother ?"

"No, indeed, I have not : and that fact more than all others, adds to my uneasiness."

"How, then, can you know anything of his afflictions."

"Because for some days past I have been in a state of great suffering myself."

"Pardon me my eternal questionings—but really to me this is inexplicable."

"Do you not know that we were twin-born."

"My guide informed me of that much."

"Have you not heard that, when we were born, we were joined together at the side ?"

"No : I was ignorant of that fact."

"Well : it was necessary to have recourse to the knife to separate us : and this remains, that,

however distant we may be from each other, even as we are now—still there is a oneness of sensation—so that whatever may be the impression, be it physical or moral, which either of us experiences or feels at any time, it produces its corresponding sensation in the body of the other. Thus, this very day, without anything occurring actually to myself to produce such a sensation, I feel dull, morose, and depressed : I feel an acute tightness and heaviness of heart. I am convinced my brother has met with some deep cause of sorrow."

I looked with astonishment at the young man, who had asserted these strange things, without seeming to have a doubt of their truth : his mother, too, seemed equally convinced of their reality.

Madame de Franchi smiled sorrowfully, and said : "The absent are in God's hands. The principal point is, that you are sure he is alive."

"If he was dead," said Lucien tranquilly, "I should have been forewarned of it."

"And thou wouldst have informed me of it, wouldst thou not, my son ?"

"At the very moment, I swear to you, my mother."

"Good. Excuse me, monsieur," said she, turning to me, "for not having in your presence put a restraint on my parental anxieties : it is not merely that Louis and Lucien are my children, but they are the last of our name. Pray seat yourself at my right : Lucien, here is your place ;" and she pointed out to the young man the vacant place on her left.

We were seated at one end of a long table; at the opposite end were covers for six, for the use of those who are designated in Corsica "the family,"—that is to say, those persons who, in large houses, hold a middle position between masters and domestics.

The table was amply provided with viands. But I must confess, that though I was as hungry as a traveller should be, I contented myself with the mere mechanical effort of satisfying my wants : my pre-occupation of mind preventing me from tasting or appreciating any of the finer or more delicate pleasures of gastronomy. In fact, I was filled with the idea that on entering this house I had immerged into a new and strange world, in which I lived as if in a dream.

Why did this lady carry a carbine like a soldier ? How could this brother feel at the same moment, the sensations of sorrow and affliction experienced by another brother who was at a distance of three hundred leagues from him ? What mother was this, who could make a son swear to divulge to her the preternatural knowledge of a second son's death ?

All this struck me forcibly, and afforded ample matter for deep cogitation. However, as I could easily understand that my silence was a breach of politeness, I raised my brow, and shook my head, as if to clear my brain from the thick-coming ideas.

The mother and son instantly saw that I wished to engage in conversation.

"And so," said Lucien to me, as if resuming an interrupted conversation, "you then decided to come to Corsica."

"Yes, as you see : in fact, I had entertained

"Then the old mother, who held the hen in her hands, twisted its neck, and, throwing it into her neighbour's face, said,
'Well, since it is your's, eat it.' "—*Page* 14.

this project for a very long period, and I have at last put it into execution."

"I'faith, you have done well not to farther delay it: for what with the invasion of French manners and tastes, those who come after you to look for Corsica will be troubled to find any traces of her."

"In any case," replied I, "if the old national spirit should recoil from before the inroads of civilization, and take refuge in some corner of the island, that spot will certainly be in the province of Sartène and in the valley of Tavaro."

"You really think so," said the young man, smiling.

"These old Corsican manners appear to me, from all that I see around, in this very spot, and under my own eyes,—to present many noble and beautiful features."

"Yes; and, notwithstanding, stepping in between my mother and myself, in spite of the traditions and memories of four hundred years, in this very house, crenated and portcullised as it is, this French spirit has come, has sought out my brother, has taken possession of him, and transported him to Paris; from whence he will return an advocate.

"He will live in Ajaccio, instead of in the house of his fathers: he will plead; and as a reward for his talents, he will perhaps be made *procureur du roi:* then he will hunt up the poor devils who have " done a skin,"* as they say in the country; he will confound assassination with murder, as you yourself did a short time since; he will demand in the name of the law, the heads of

* *Fait une peau.*

"We sat, or rather laid down on a turfy slope facing an immense breach in the walls."—*Page* 18.

those who have but done what their forefathers would have considered the deepest dishonour not to have done; he will substitute man's judgment against the judgment of God; and at night, after having sent another head to the scaffold, he will believe that he has nobly served his country—that he has added a stone to the Temple of Civilization; as our prefect would say. Ah, my God! my God!" And here the young man lifted up his eyes to Heaven, like Hannibal after the battle of Zama.

"But," responded I, "you can readily perceive that God has wisely counterbalanced those tendencies: since, though your brother is imbued with a love of those new principles, you are as warm a partisan of the old system."

"Yes: but who will say that my brother will not follow his uncle's example rather than that of mine; and for myself, am I not left to follow a line of conduct unworthy of a De Franchi?"

"You!" I exclaimed, in astonishment.

"Ah! my God! yes—I. Shall I tell you what you are come in pursuit of in the province of Sartène?"

"Say on."

"You have come here with the curiosity of a man of the world, of an artist—or of a poet—I know not what you are, neither do I ask you: you may tell us before leaving, if it so please you, if not, you are our guest, you may keep silent—you are perfectly free. Well, you have come to this country in the hope of seeing some village in a state of *vendetta*; you wish to come in contact with some original of a bandit, such as M. Mérimée has depicted in 'Colomba.'"

"Well—well—it would appear as if I had not made a very great mistake, for either my eyes deceive me, or your house is the only one in the village which is not fortified as if for a siege."

"That itself proves that I also am degenerated: my father, grandfather, great grandfather—any and every one of my ancestors, took the part of one or other of the two factions which have divided this village for so many years. Well—do you know what I am—amidst all these musket-shots, dagger-stabs, and knife-thrusts—I am an arbitrator! You have come to the province of Sartène to see the bandits, have you not? Good. Come with me to-night, and I will show you one?"

"How! will you allow me to accompany you?"

"Oh, by Jove! yes: if it will amuse you; there is nothing to hinder."

"Then I gladly accept your offer."

"Monsieur is too much fatigued," said Madame de Franchi, with a glance at her son, as if she participated in the shame he experienced in feeling himself, a Corsican, so degenerated.

"No, mother, no; on the contrary, it is necessary he should come with me: so that, at a future time perhaps, when he hears in some Parisian saloon, people talk of those terrible *vendettas*, or of those implacable Corsican bandits, who are even now the terror of the little children of Bartia and Ajaccio,—at the least he will be able to shrug his shoulders and speak of what he has seen."

"But what can originate those great quarrels, which, as far as I can judge from what you have told me, are now all but extinguished?"

"Oh!" said Lucien, "in a quarrel, it is not the cause which does the business, it is the effect. If a fly in its flight causes a man's death, he is not the less a dead man, even though a fly be the cause."

I saw from his manner that he himself hesitated to inform me of the origin of this terrible civil war, which had for ten years desolated the village of Sullacaro. But, the more reluctant he seemed to divulge it, the more eager was I to extort it.

"Nevertheless," said I, "this quarrel had a first cause. Is its origin a secret?"

"My God! no. The thing had its birth between the Orlandi and the Colona."

"Upon what occasion?"

"You shall hear. A hen, escaping from the court-yard of the Orlandi, flew into that of the Colona. The Orlandi went to reclaim the hen: the Colona insisted that it was their own; the Orlandi threatened to bring them before the justice of peace, and make oath before him. Then the old mother, who held the hen in her hands, twisted its neck, and throwing it into her neighbour's face, said, 'Well, since it is your's, eat it!' Immediately an Orlandi took up the hen by its feet, and was about to hurl it at the old dame who had thrown it in his sister's face: but, at the moment he raised his arm, a Colona, who, by some ill-luck had a loaded gun in his hand, sent a ball through his body, and killed him on the spot."

"And how many lives have been sacrificed since this scuffle?"

"There have been nine killed."

"And all this for a miserable fowl, worth about twelve sous!"

"Undoubtedly: but I told you, just now, that these affairs were not to be judged by their origin but from their results."

"And because there have been nine lives lost, it will necessarily follow there will be a tenth?"

"You will see there will not," replied Lucien: "since I am made arbitrator."

"Of course at the request of a member of one or other of the two families?"

"Oh, my God, no! it is at my brother's instance, who heard of the affair at the house of the keeper of the seals. I would ask you one little question,—why the devil do they trouble themselves in Paris with what passes in a little miserable Corsican village? It is that prefect who has played us this turn, boasting that if I would but say the word, the whole thing would finish like a vaudeville, by a public marriage and a couplet of verses: then he addresses himself to my brother, who, catching the ball at the rebound, writes to me and tells me that he has pledged his word for me. What could I do?" said the young man, raising his head; "it would not do to let them say below that one of the Franchi had pledged his word for his brother, and that that brother had dishonoured the engagement!"

"Then it is all arranged."

"I am afraid so."

"And there is no doubt but that we shall see to-night the chief of one of the two factions?"

"Exactly—last night I had an interview with the other."

"Is it an Orlandi or a Colona that we go to visit this evening?"

"An Orlandi."

"How far is the rendezvous from here?"

"At the ruined Castle of Vicentello d'Istria!"

"Ah! true! I have heard that those ruins were in the environs of the village."

"About a league hence."

"In that case, we shall be there in about three quarters of an hour's time or little more?"

"Rather more."

"Lucien," said Madame de Franchi, "recollect that thou art speaking for thyself. Thou, a mountaineer, canst scarcely get there in three-quarters of an hour, but this gentleman can not go the way thou wouldst go."

"That is true: it will take us an hour and a half at least to get there."

"You have no time to lose," said the lady, casting her eyes towards the timepiece.

"Mother," said Lucien: "will you permit us to withdraw?"

She extended to him her hand: the young man bowed and kissed it with the same respectful homage he had shewn on his entrance.

"Seriously," said Lucien to me, "if you would really prefer to digest your supper tranquilly, you have only to ascend to your chamber, warm your legs by the fire, and smoke your cigar?"

"No—no—decidedly no. The devil! you have promised me a bandit, and I must have it."

"Good—let us then take our guns, and be off on our road."

Making my respectful salutations to Madame de Franchi, we left the room, preceded by Griffo, with a light. Our preparations were very soon made. I bound a traveller's belt which I had brought from Paris around my waist; to which hung a sort of hunting-knife, or *couteau de chasse*; on one side of my sash was a deposit for powder: on the other was a shot pouch. As for Lucien he reappeared from his room with his cartouche-box slung around him, a double-barrelled Joe Manton in his hands and a pointed cap, the embroidery on which was no doubt the master-piece of some fair Penelope of Sullacaro.

"Shall I go with your Excellence?" asked Griffo.

"No: it is unnecessary," replied Lucien; "but you will let Diamond loose; it may possibly happen that we may rouse a pheasant, and with this moonlight, we could take aim as if it were mid-day." As he was speaking, a large spaniel dog bounded and barked around us for sheer joy.

We had not gone more than a dozen paces from the house, when Lucien urned and said to Griffo—"By-the-by, you may as well make our departure known in the village, so that, in case they should hear the sound of fire-arms in the mountains, they may know the reason."

"Make yourself easy on that head, Excellence," responded Griffo.

"Without this precaution," replied Lucien, "they might fancy that hostilities had recommenced; and the sound of our fire-arms might be echoed by that of musketry in the streets of Sullacaro." After proceeding a few yards along the principal street, we turned into a narrow lane on our right which led directly to the mountains.

CHAPTER VI.

ALTHOUGH it was now but the beginning of March, the weather was magnificent: indeed, it might be termed hot, were it not for the lovely and refreshing breeze, which brought with it the sharp and invigorating odour of the sea. The moon rose, clear and brilliant, behind Mont de Cagna; pouring, so to speak, floods of light upon the western line of boundary which separates Corsica into two parts, and in a manner making of one island two different countries, eternally at war, or at all events, in a state of enmity against each other. As we advanced, and whilst the deep gorges or the frowning top of Tavaro plunged all things immediately around us into a depth of darkness, the obscurity of which the eye sought in vain to penetrate, we could see the calm Mediterranean, appearing like a vast mirror of burnished steel extending to the verge of the horizon. Those strange and peculiar noises of the night, which disappear and give place to others during the day, but which may truly be said to awaken to life with the approach of night, now made themselves heard; and produced—not upon Lucien, who was familiar with them, and could recognize and trace each to its cause—but upon me, to whom they were strange and unwonted, a singular combination of awe and surprise; and kept my mind in a continual emotion, giving an interest to everything which I saw or heard.

On our arrival at a species of branch road, which here separated into two—namely, a road which appeared to wind around the mountain, and a narrow path which was just visible on the right, Lucien stopped.

"One word," said he to me. "Have you got a mountaineer's foot?"

"I have the feet, Monsieur; but not the eye."

"That is to say, you are subject to vertigo."

"Yes—the sight of a chasm affects me irresistibly."

"Then we will take the bridle path; by this we shall avoid the precipices, and shall only encounter the difficulties of the path."

"Oh! I am equal to any amount of difficulty on fair ground."

"And taking this path: it will save us three quarter's of an hour's walking."

"The path be it, then."

Lucien's first occupation was to plunge into a little thicket of green oaks, where I followed. Diamond trotted on at about fifty or sixty paces ahead, beating the wood right and left, and from time to time returning by the path, joyfully wagging his tail, as if to announce to us that we might, without any danger, and implicitly confiding in his instinct, quietly follow our route. In fact, like the double-action horses of those half fashionables, brokers on Change by day, fast men by night, and who make of the same animal a saddle horse and a cabriolet hack—Diamond was equally up to his business, whether hunting the biped or the quadruped; the bandit or the wolf.

Not caring to have the appearance of one totally ignorant of Corsican manners, I imparted to Lucien my observations.

"You are mistaken," replied he. "Diamond does indeed effectually hunt men as well as brutes, but the men he pursues are not bandits: they are included in the triple classes of gendarme, soldier, and volunteer."

"How! Diamond is then a bandit's dog?"

"You have said so. Diamond belonged to an Orlandi, to whom I used to send at times, whilst in the country, powder, bullets, and a few other necessaries which a bandit is occasionally in want of. He was killed by a Colona; and the day after I took charge of his dog, which, having been in the habit of coming to our house, very soon became attached to me."

"But I think that, looking from my chamber, or rather I should have said from your brother's, I saw another dog."

"Yes: that was Brusco: he possesses exactly the same qualities, and came to me under the same circumstances as this dog: only with this difference, Brusco's master was a Colona, who was killed by an Orlandi. Hence, it follows, that when I go to visit one of the Colona, I take Brusco with me: when, on the contrary, I have any business to do with an Orlandi, I am accompanied by Diamond. If they were by any accident set loose at the same time, they would destroy each other. Men," continued Lucien, with his peculiar bitter smile, "when they wish to be reconciled with each other, communicate from the same host,—these dogs can never be brought to eat from the same dish."

"Well, well!" replied I, laughing, "at all events they are true Corsican dogs: but it seems to me that Diamond, like a modest dog as he is, has robbed himself of our commendations; for ever since the conversation began to turn on his good qualities, he has been missing."

"Don't let that trouble you," said Lucien, "I know where he is gone."

"And where is that, if I may ask the question?"

"Orlandi was a man of tall stature, wearing his beard at its full growth, and dressed precisely in the same fashion as the young Franchi."—*Page* 19.

"He is at the *mucchio*."*

I was about to ask for an explanation, even at the risk of fatiguing my companion, when I was startled by a howl so sad, prolonged, and melancholy, that I involuntarily stopped, and placing my hand on Lucien's arm, exclaimed—

"What— whatever is that ?"

"Nothing, it is only Diamond lamenting."

"And for whom is he lamenting?"

"His master. Think you, then, that dogs are like men, and forget those whom they have loved ?"

* *Mucchio*—The Corsican term for the mound or cairn formed by the continued deposit, by passers by, of boughs or stones on the spot where a murder has taken place. A similar custom prevails in Ireland ; where each person passing by the *locale* of a murder, throws a stone on the spot and mutters a prayer for the repose of the victim's soul.—*Trans.*

"Ah, I understand," said I. Diamond howled a second time in a tone more sad, more prolonged, and more melancholy than the first.

"Yes," said I: "I understand. His master was killed, as you have informed me, and we are approaching the spot where he was murdered."

"Exactly ; and Diamond has quitted us to go to the *mucchio*."

"The mucchio, then, is the tomb of the deceased ?"

"Yes: that is to say, a monument erected by each person who passes by throwing a stone and a branch of a tree upon the spot where the man was assassinated. It follows, that instead of the tomb being effaced by the tread of that great universal leveller, Time, the monument raised to the victim increases daily—a symbol of that thirst for vengeance which survives him, and

POUGET   OSEQUIN

"We gained a sort of natural platform, upon which stood some ruined walls."—Page 18.

which grows incessantly in the hearts of his kinsmen."

A third time the howl was heard: and this time it was so near to us, that I could not help feeling a sensation of chilliness and fear, though now I was perfectly cognizant of the cause.

In fact, at a turn of the path, I saw, at about twenty paces from us a white mound of stones, forming a pyramid of some four or five feet in height. This was the *mucchio.*

At the foot of this strange monument sat Diamond, with neck outstretched, and mouth open. Lucien took up a stone, and taking off his cap, approached the *mucchio.*

I did the same: in fact, taking his actions for my model in every respect.

On arriving near the pyramid, he broke off a branch of green oak,—and threw on the mound first the stone, afterwards the branch: finally he rapidly crossed himself,—a custom truly Corsican, and one which even Napoleon himself was often seen to do under peculiar or terrible circumstances.

I imitated him exactly. Then, silent and pensive, we resumed our travel.

About ten minutes afterwards, we heard a last howl, and immediately afterwards Diamond, who had again returned to his occupation as a scout, passed about a hundred paces from us.

CHAPTER VII.

Meanwhile we proceeded on our road: and, as I had been forewarned by Lucien, the path became more and more precipitous and rugged. As I could see plainly that I should soon have sufficient occupation for both hands, I slung my carbine. But as for my guide, he marched on with perfect ease, nor seemed to be aware that there was any difficulty in traversing the rugged path. After some minutes of climbing and traversing the rocky defiles, somewhat aided in our progress by bindweed and the roots of trees, we gained a sort of natural platform, upon which stood some ruined remains of walls. They formed part of the ruins of the Castle of Vicentello d'Istria,—which was the end of our journey. Another five minutes of escalading, over rocks and hillocks still more difficult to surmount than the first stage, and Lucien, on attaining the last of a succession of these platforms or terraces, extended his arm, and taking hold of my hand, exclaimed—

"Come, come ; you don't travel badly for a Parisian."

"The reason is—because the Parisian to whom you have just lent your aid to make his last stride, has already taken a few excursions of the same sort."

"Yes, yes," said Lucien, laughing. "Have you not near Paris a mountain which they call Montmartre?"

"Yes: but besides Montmartre, which I admit, I have scrambled up a few other mountains, —namely, the Righi, Vesuvius, Stromboli, Etna, and others."

"Ah! now, on the other hand, it is you who have the laugh at me, for I have never climbed but the Monte-Rotondo. In any case, here we are on the spot where for four hundred years my ancestors kept open doors, and have said: 'Welcome to our castle!' To-day, their descendant, standing amid its ruins, says to you: 'Welcome to our ruins.'"

"Has this castle then been in your family ever since the death of Vicentello d'Istria?" asked I, taking up the conversation at the point we had left off.

"No: but before his birth it was the abode of an ancestress of ours, the famous Savilia, widow of Lucien de Franchi."

"Have they not, in Philippini, a terrible legend of this lady?"

"Yes. If it were daylight, you could see from this spot the ruins of the Castle of Valle. Here was the dwelling-place of the Seigneur de Giudice—a man as universally hated as Savilia was generally beloved—as ugly as the lady was beautiful. He became enamoured of her, and as she seemed in no great hurry to reciprocate his ardent passion, he gave her to understand that if she did not accept him for her spouse within a given time, he would carry her off by force. Savilia made a pretence of acceding to his wishes, and politely invited her would-be-husband to dine with her, at her château. Giudice, overwhelmed with joy, and forgetting that he had arrived at this flattering result only by the aid of his threats, hastened to the castle accompanied only by a few servants. The door was closed behind them on their arrival, and five minutes after, the ardent lover, Giudice, found himself safely enclosed in a dungeon."

Taking the direction indicated by Lucien, I found myself in a sort of square court. Through the breaches made by time in the walls streamed the bright rays of the moon over the rubbish-encumbered ground, whilst other portions of the inclosure and building remained deep-hidden in the shadow of the walls which surrounded them.

Lucien took out his watch.

"Ah!" said he, "we are twenty minutes before our time. Sit down, you are no doubt somewhat tired."

We sat, or rather laid down on a turfy slope facing an immense breach in the walls.

"You have not told me the whole of Savilia's story," said I to Lucien.

"No," replied he, and continued. "Every morning and evening Savilia descended to the dungeon in which her quondam lover was immured, and there displayed, separated from him only by a grating, her unrobed charms to the gaze of her captive. 'Giudice,' she would say to him, 'how is it that a man so ugly as thou art, should have ever believed that thou could'st become the possessor of a woman so beautiful as her thou now seest.' This punishment she renewed twice a day, for three months—at morn and eve. But at the end of that period, thanks to a servant-girl whom he had seduced, Giudice escaped from his incarceration. Burning with hatred, he returned with all his vassals, which far outnumbered those of Savilia, took the castle by storm, and Savilia, made prisoner in her turn, was stripped and exposed in a large iron cage, placed in a cross-road in the forest of Bocca di Cilaccia ; Giudice was himself the gaoler, and with his own hands proffered the key to any passer-by whom her beauty might attract. After three months of this atrocious public prostitution, Savilia died."

"Eh, bien," responded I: "it appears to me that your ancestors were well versed in the luxury of vengeance ; and that, in destroying each other so summarily by musket-ball or dagger-thrust, their descendants have a little degenerated."

"You have not counted on the fact that after all it comes to the same. But, at all events, the feeling did not pass away in our family. The two sons of Savilia, who were at the time at Ajaccio, under the care of their uncle, immediately took up arms, and continued to wage war against the sons of Giudice. This war lasted for four centuries, and was not finished until, as you might have seen inscribed on the carbines of my parents, the 21st September, 1819, at one o'clock in the morning."

"In fact, that brings to my recollection this inscription you alluded to, of which I was very anxious to ask you the explanation, but at the moment I was called on to descend to dine."

"Here it is, then. In 1819 only two brothers remained of the whole race of Giudice : of the family of Franchi my father was the sole survivor ; he married his cousin. Three months after their marriage, the brothers Giudice resolved by one grand blow to put an end to the war between the two races. One of the brothers laid an ambuscade upon the road to Olmedo, waiting for my father on his return from Sartène; while the other, taking advantage of his absence from home, was to assail our house. The affair was put in operation according to the plan proposed: but the event turned out contrary to the expectations of the aggressors. My father, forewarned, was on his guard; my mother, having had intimation of their project, assembled the shepherds: so that at the moment of the double attack, each of my parents were in a state of defence. After five minutes of sharp conflict, the brothers Giudice fell—one by the bullet of my father—the other from the carbine shot of my mother. On seeing the enemy of his house fall, my father took out his watch, It was *one o'clock!* And when my mother saw her adversary was no more, she turned towards the *pendule* on the mantel-piece; it was *one o'clock*. All was finished at the same moment of time: henceforward there existed no trace of the Giudice: the race was extinct. The Franchi, thus victorious, was from that time tranquil, and as this had put a stop to a civil war which had raged during four centuries, there was nothing further to implicate the family in bloodshed. But my father thought proper to have the inscriptions you allude to engraved on the butt-ends of the carbines which had been the instruments of putting an end to the warfare: and they have ever since hung one on each side of the time-piece, as you have yourself seen them. Seven months after this, my mother brought into the world twin-sons: your humble servant, the Corsican Lucien, is one of them; the other is the philanthropist Louis, his brother."

As he finished, I saw, by the aid of a sudden gleam of moonlight, the shadows of a man and dog approaching us. They were caused by the bandit Orlandi, and our friend Diamond.

At that moment the town-clock of Sullacaro struck nine.

Master Orlandi was, as it appeared, of a similar opinion with Louis XIV., who held, as they say, that punctuality was a royal virtue; for it was impossible to be more exact to time than was this king of the mountains.

On perceiving him, we both arose.

CHAPTER VIII.

"You have not come here alone, M. Lucien?" said the bandit.

"Don't trouble yourself about that, Orlandi; Monsieur is a friend of mine, who has heard you spoken of, and who wished to pay you a visit. I did not believe you would refuse him the pleasure."

"Monsieur is welcome to the country," said the bandit, bowing and advancing some steps towards us.

I returned his salutation with the most punctilious politeness.

"You have been waiting some time?" said Orlandi.

"Yes—twenty minutes."

"About that: I heard Diamond howling at the *mucchio*, and a quarter of an hour afterwards the dog joined me. It is a good and faithful animal, is it not, M. Lucien?"

"Yes—those are the very words—good and faithful," replied Lucien, caressing the dog.

"But, since you were aware that M. Lucien was here awaiting you, why not have come sooner?" demanded I.

"Because the time of rendezvous was fixed at nine o'clock, and it would have been just as much a lack of punctuality to have been a quarter of an hour before as to have been a quarter of an hour behind time."

"Is that reproof intended for me?" asked Lucien.

"No, sir; you might have particular reasons for being early: besides you were accompanied by your friend, and it is probably on his account that you have departed from your accustomed habit, for you are always to the minute, M. Lucien, and I know that better than any one, for often have you inconvenienced yourself for me."

"You will not have that to boast of long, Orlandi, for in all probability this will be the last time."

"Have we not a few words to exchange on that subject, M. Lucien?" asked the bandit.

"Yes; and if you will follow me"—

"I am at your orders."

Lucien then turned towards me, and said, "You will please excuse me for a short time?"

They both retired to a short distance, and mounting one of the breaches by which Orlandi had entered, they both turned round, so that their features were thrown out in the full light of the moon, which, as it were, bathed their bronzed countenances in a flood of silvery light. It was then that I could attentively examine Orlandi; he was a man of tall stature, wearing his beard at its full growth, and dressed precisely in the same fashion as the young Franchi, with this exception, that the clothes of the former bore more trace of frequent contact with the marshy forests of which he was the lord, of the briars through which, more than once, he had scrambled in flight, and of the ground which he had many a night made his couch.

I could understand nothing of their conversation—in the first place because they were at a distance from me of twenty yards, in the next, because they spoke in the Corsican dialect. But I could very easily comprehend from his violent gesticulations that the bandit disputed, with very great heat, a course of reasoning which the young man unfolded with a calm dignity which did honour to his character as an arbitrator. After some time, the gesticulations of the Orlandi became less frequent if not less energetic, his speech seemed to languish; after a last observation, he bowed down his head—then, after a moment's silence, held out his hand to the young man. The conference, in all probability, was now concluded: for they both came towards me.

"My dear guest," said the young man to me, "Orlandi wishes to thank you."

"For what?" asked I.

"For having the kindness to become one of his sponsors. I have pledged my word for that much."

"A contemptuous smile curled the lips of the bandit."—*Page* 20.

"If you have done so, of course you will understand that I accept it, though I have no knowledge of what the affair is." So saying, I held out my hand to the bandit, who did me the honour to touch it with the tip of his finger.

"You will do this much—you will inform my brother that everything is arranged according to his desire, and that you have signed the contract."

"Will there be a marriage, then?"

"No: not yet, but perhaps that may follow."

A contemptuous smile curled the lips of the bandit, as he replied:

"Peace there may be, since you absolutely require it; but never alliance: that is not n the treaty."

"No," said Lucien, "it is only in all probability written in the future. But let us change the subject. Did you not hear something whilst I was engaged in conversation with Orlandi?"

"Do you mean of what you were talking?"

"No; but a pheasant talking in the neighbouring thicket.

"On recollection, I did hear something like the crowing of a pheasant, but I believed myself to have been mistaken."

"No mistake at all: there is a cock pheasant roosting in the great chestnut tree, you know, Monsieur Lucien, about a hundred yards from this spot. I have heard him at intervals for the last hour."

"Turning himself round, he saw his brother, with his hand resting on his own shoulder."—*Page 26.*

"Good—good," said Lucien gaily, "he shall form part of our dinner to-morrow."

"I would have brought him down long before this," said Orlandi, "if I had not been afraid that they might believe at the village it was something more serious than pheasant shooting."

"I have forewarned them," said Lucien. "*Apropos* of shooting," added he, turning himself towards me, and throwing his piece on his shoulder, "the privilege is yours."

"Another time: I am doubtless not so good a shot as you are, and I have a great wish to eat my part of the pheasant—so bring him down yourself."

"Very likely, if you have not experience in night sporting, you would fire too low; to-morrow, if you have nothing else to do, you can take your turn."

CHAPTER IX.

We left the ruins by the side opposite to where we had entered them—Lucien taking the lead. Almost directly we had entered the thicket, the pheasant, as if desirous of being his own betrayer, began to crow. The bird was about eighty yards from where we were, hidden from our sight in the dense branches of a chesnut tree, the approach to which was defended by a thicket of thorns.

".How can you get a shot at him, without hearing him at the time," asked I; "that appears to me not an easy job."

"No :" he answered, "if I can get a sight of him, I can bring him down from where I stand."

"What! from here? will your piece kill at eighty yards?"

"With small shot, no : with a bullet, yes."

"Ah! with a ball—that is another affair, and yet you will do well to bring him down at a shot."

"Have you the sight?" asked Orlandi.

"Yes," said Lucien, "I have it just to my liking."

"Look out, then!" and Orlandi began to imitate the clucking of a hen pheasant. At the same moment, without seeing the pheasant we perceived a movement amidst the foliage of the chestnut tree: the pheasant mounted branch after branch, still responding to the clucking made by Orlandi, until he gained the summit of the tree, where he was perfectly visible—standing out in bold relief from the dead white of the sky. Orlandi ceased his imitative clucking, and the pheasant remained immoveable, and immediately Lucien lowered his piece, took a momentary glance at the bird, and fired. The pheasant fell like lead.

"Go—find him!" said Lucien to Diamond. The dog entered the thicket, and five minutes after reappeared with the pheasant in his mouth. On inspection, we found the ball had gone clear through his body.

"A capital shot that," said I. "I must indeed compliment you on your skill with the double-barrel."

"Oh," said Lucien, "there is not so much skill in the affair as you imagine : one of the barrels is grooved and will carry a ball as true as a rifle."

"No matter for that ; such a shot, even with a rifle, is deserving of honourable mention."

"Bah!" said Orlandi—"M. Lucien can, with a rifle-shot, hit a five-franc piece at a hundred yards."

"Are you an adept with the pistol as well as with the gun."

"At a less distance : set up a knife endways, and at twenty-five yards I can count upon splitting six out of every twelve balls I fire at the edge of it."

I took off my hat, and saluted Lucien.

"And is your brother equally skilled in this respect?"

"My brother!" exclaimed he, "poor Louis! He never in his life touched gun or pistol. I am continually worried by the apprehension of his getting into some scrape or other at Paris. In that case, his courage and his love of country will be his death."

So saying, Lucien deposited the slain pheasant in his pocket.

"Now, my dear Orlandi, to-morrow."

"To-morrow, Monsieur Lucien."

"I know your punctuality: at ten o'clock, you, your friends and your sponsors, will all be at the end of the street—that, I believe, is the arrangement. At the foot of the mountain, at the same hour, and at the opposite end of the street, Colona will be found, on his side, with all his friends and sponsors. Then we shall all walk to the church."

"You have said right, Monsieur Lucien ; I thank you for your trouble. And you, sir," continued Orlandi, turning round and saluting me, "I thank you for the honour."

With these compliments, we separated : Orlandi to retire to his wild domain, and we to take the road to the village. As for Diamond, he seemed to be in a state of indecision which party to follow—alternately fixing his gaze on Orlandi and on us. Finally, after some five minutes' hesitation, he honored us by his preference.

I will acknowledge that it was with no small amount of anxiety, that I thought upon our descent down the face of the double platform of rocks which I had escalated—well aware that the descent is far more difficult, generally speaking, than the ascent. I was not sorry, therefore, when Lucien, as if divining my thoughts, struck into a path different from that by which we had come. This change of route afforded another advantage—it was that of conversation, a thing totally impossible to be carried on with any amount of ease whilst the ascent of straight and precipitous ledges of rock occupied one's whole attention. So, as the declivities were gradual, and the road easy, I had not proceeded more than a few steps, ere I fell into my old habit of asking questions.

"So, then, peace is concluded?" said I.

"Yes, but as you must have perceived, it was not without some trouble. In fact, I had to make him understand that all the advances towards reconciliation were made by the Colona. Besides the latter had had five men killed during the vendetta, whilst the Orlandi had only lost four. The Colona gave their consent to a reconciliation yesterday, whilst the Orlandi only consented at this moment. Finally, the Colona have engaged publicly to give a living fowl to the Orlandi—a concession which goes to prove that they were in the wrong from the first. The last consideration was the finishing stroke."

"And to-morrow this touching reconciliation is to take place?"

"At ten o'clock to-morrow : you will see that you are not so very unlucky after all. You wished to see a vendetta!" The young man again resumed with one of his bitter smiles : "Bah! it is a fine thing that vendetta! During four hundred years Corsica has heard no one speak of anything else ; but you will see a reconciliation, which is a wonderful rare thing to see—far more rare than a vendetta."

I laughed.

"You laugh at us, and you have good reason for so doing—we are, in sober truth, the most ridiculous of mankind."

"No," said I, "I laughed at something very different : to think that you, who are so furious a partisan, should have so well succeeded as an arbitrator."

"Is it not strange? Ah: if you could but have understood me, you would have admired my eloquence. But come here ten years hence, and you may be assured that everybody will speak French."

"You are an excellent pleader."

"Not at all: understand, I am an arbitrator. What the deuce could I do? If they were to make me arbitrator betwixt the blessed St. Michael and Satan, I would use my utmost endeavours to reconcile them, even though, at the bottom of my heart, I was convinced that in listening to me St. Michael would be making a fool of himself."

Seeing that this conversation only served to make my companion angry, I dropped the subject; and as he did not make any advances towards taking it up, we arrived at the house without either of us speaking a word more.

CHAPTER X.

GRIFFO waited on us. Before his master had spoken a word to him, Griffo had investigated Lucien's pocket, and had drawn from it the pheasant. He had heard and recognised the sound of fire-arms.

Madame de Franchi had not yet gone to bed, but had retired to her chamber, charging Griffo to request her son to confer with her before he retired to rest.

The young man having inquired if his guest wanted anything, and having been answered by me in the negative, asked permission of absence in order to obey the wishes of his mother. I bade him a good night, and ascended to my chamber.

It was not without pleasure that I reviewed the day's proceedings. My analytical studies had not misled me, and I felt elated at having divined the character of Louis equally with that of Lucien. Thus congratulating myself, I slowly undressed myself, and having taken the *Orientale* of Victor Hugo from the book-case of the future lawyer, I threw myself on my couch, in as happy a mood as man need be in. I had just began reading, for the hundredth time, the *Feu du Ciel*, when I heard some one ascending the stairs, and stop at my door, at which I heard a very gentle knock. I had not the least doubt that this was my host, who had come with the intention to wish me good night, but who, thinking that I might have been already asleep, hesitated to open the door.

"Come in!" said I, laying my book down on the table.

Immediately the door was opened by Lucien.

"Excuse me," said he, "but it has struck me on reflection that I have behaved unhandsomely to you to-night, and I could not retire to my couch before asking your pardon. I have come, then, to make an apology, and, as you appear to have still many questions to propound, I am now at your entire disposal."

"Many thanks, but, owing to your kindness, I have been so far instructed in all that I wished to know, that there is only one thing left which I have resolved never to inquire concerning."

"Why not?"

"Because it would really be too indiscreet. Meanwhile I will give you warning not to press the subject, as I will not in that case answer for myself."

"Good! now go on as fast as you please. It is a bad thing that unsatisfied curiosity, it leads naturally to surmises, and out of every three of such surmises you will find two to be far more prejudicial to the person who is the object of them than the whole truth could possibly be."

"Rest your mind contented on that score: my most injurious surmises, as far as you are concerned, would lead me only to believe that you were a sorcerer."

The young man laughed.

"The devil!" exclaimed he, "you will make me more curious than yourself. Go on, it is I who beg you to answer now?"

"Well, you have had the goodness to explain to me everything that is obscure saving on one point. You have showed me those weapons, historically valuable, which I now ask your permission once more to review before I depart"—

"That is one."

"You have explained to me the signification of the inscriptions—alike in words and effect—on the stock of the carbines"—

"That is the second."

"You have made me acquainted with the fact that owing to the phenomena attending your birth, you experience, although separated from your brother by a distance of three hundred leagues, the same sensations as himself—and which are doubtless reciprocated in the same manner on his part"—

"That is the third."

"But when Madame de Franchi, *apropos* of the uneasiness of your mind, which led you to a belief that some evil had threatened or troubled your brother, asked of you if you were certain that he was alive, you replied 'Yes, if he was dead, I should have been warned of it'"—

"Yes, that is true; I did indeed say those words."

"Well, if an explanation of those words may be committed to profane ears, I pray you to explain them to me."

The young man's countenance assumed, as I spoke, such a grave and sombre expression, that I hesitated in pronouncing the last words. For a moment after I had ceased speaking there was a dead silence.

"Hold!" said I to him, "I can well see that I have been, to say the least, indiscreet. Think I have said nothing on the subject."

"No—no!" said he: "only, you are a man of the world, and, consequently, you are somewhat incredulous on those points. Well, I fear you will treat as an idle superstition an ancient family tradition which has been implicitly believed by us for four hundred years."

"Listen!" said I to him. "I solemnly declare to you, that no one, as regards legends or traditions, can be more credulous than myself; and in the same way with other things which I believe more particularly—that is, things seemingly impossible."

"Then you believe in apparitions?"

"What would you say if I tell you that I myself am a witness to the fact—that the thing has happened to me."

"Yes—that would justify and encourage me."

"My father died in 1807—when I was scarcely three and a half years of age. As the doctor had told our friends that his end was very near, they

Colona.—*Page 27.*

carried me away to an old cousin, who lived in a house situate between the court-yard and garden. She had made me up a bed close to her own: and I was put to rest at the usual time, and notwithstanding the threatened loss of my parents—a loss which my age prevented me from fully appreciating—I slept soundly. I was awakened suddenly by three violent knocks at the door of the bedchamber; I got out of my bed, and was making my way towards the door.

"'Where art thou going?' asked my cousin, who had, with myself, been awakened by the triple knock at the door. As she well knew that the street door was locked, and that consequently no one could enter to knock at the inner door, she was not able to master a certain fear and dread on the occasion.

"'I am going to open the door to papa, who is come to bid me farewell.'

"It was her turn to jump out of her bed, and in spite of my tears and struggles, to place me in my bed. I cried loudly and continually, 'Papa is at the door, and I will see papa before he goes away for ever.'"

"Has the appearance ever been renewed?" asked Lucien.

"No: though I have often wished for it. But perhaps, God granted to the purity of the child, what he denies to the corruption of the man."

"Ah!" said Lucien to me, smiling, "our

"By an instinctive movement the two enemies carried their hands behind them."—*Page* 27.

family are more gifted in that respect than yours."

"Do you see your parents after their death ?"

"On every occasion when some great event is about to happen, or after it is accomplished."

"And to what do you attribute this privilege so accorded to your race ?"

"I will give you here the tradition which has been kept by our family. I have told you that Savilia died, leaving two sons."

"Yes : I recollect you did."

"These two sons grew up, loving each other with all the love which they could have possibly borne towards their parents, had their parents lived. They took an oath to each other that

nothing should ever separate them, not even death itself. And, after I know not what species of powerful conjuration, they wrote upon parchment with their blood the oath which they had reciprocally taken—that the first who died should appear to the other, first, at the moment of his death, and afterwards at every important event during the life of the other. Those parchments, thus written, they exchanged. Three months afterwards, one of the two brothers was killed in an ambuscade, at a moment when the other was engaged in sealing a letter which he was about to send to his brother; when, as he was about to apply the seal to the still burning wax, he heard some one sigh behind him : and, on turning himself round, he saw his brother with his hand resting on his own shoulder, though he could not feel the weight of his arm. By an involuntary movement he held out the letter which he was about to dispatch; his brother took the letter and vanished. Doubtless the two brothers had engaged not only for themselves, but also for their descendants, for, ever since that period, those appearances take place, not only at the passing hour of the dying, but also on the occasion of any great or important phase or circumstance in life."

"Have you ever seen the apparition?"

"No: but as my father, on the night previous to his death, was forewarned of the coming event by my grandfather, I presume that we—that is my brother and I, inherit the privilege of our ancestors, not having done anything to renounce this peculiarity."

"Is the privilege confined to the male portion of the family?"

"It is."

"That is strange."

"It is—so far."

I gazed at the young man as he spoke—coldly, gravely, and calmly—of things accounted impossibilities, and I repeated with Hamlet,

"There are more things 'twixt heaven and earth, Horatio,
    Than are dreamt of in thy philosophy."

At Paris I should have taken the young man for a mystifier, a fanatic, or charlatan: but in the depths of Corsica, in a little unknown village, it was necessary to consider whether he was one whose ignorance had made him the victim of credulity, or whether he was a man really invested with an attribute which might make him either the most fortunate or the most unlucky of mankind.

"Now," said he to me, after a somewhat long silence, "do you now know all you wish?"

"Yes, I thank you. I am deeply touched by your confidence in me, and I promise you to keep the secret faithfully."

"Ah, my God!" said he, with his peculiar smile "there is no secret in it; the first person you meet in the village will tell you the story as I have related it to you. One thing I hope, that is, that my brother will never boast of this circumstance at Paris, for in that case he will most probably be laughed at to his face by the men, whilst he will shock the nerves of the ladies."

So saying he rose, wished me good night, and retired to his room.

Though much fatigued, it was some time before I could compose myself to sleep, and my slumbers were anything but peaceful. In my dreams, I jumbled confusedly all the persons with whom I had been in company during my sojourn: all formed an incongruous mixture of persons and circumstances. It was near daylight before I could be said fairly to sleep, and I did not awake until the sound of the village clock struck on my ears. I took hold of the bell-pull—for my luxurious predecessor had provided himself with this, which I believe was the only thing of the sort existing in the village. Almost immediately Griffo appeared, hot water in hand. Lucien, he informed me, had already asked twice if I was arisen, and had expressed his determination to call on me at half-past nine, if I did not make an appearance before that time.

It was now five and twenty minutes past nine, so I had not long to wait for his appearance.

On this occasion M. Lucien was elegantly dressed in the French style; he wore a black frock coat, a fancy vest, and white trousers, for, even in the beginning of March, it is fashionable in Corsica to wear white.

He saw that I looked at him with some degree of surprise.

"You wonder at my appearance," said he to me: "it is a new proof of our coming civilization."

"Yes, on my word, I must confess that I am not a little astonished to find you have so finished a tailor in Ajaccio. Why, in my velveteen I shall look a complete John of Paris by the side of you."

"My costume is the handiwork of Humann,* every article of it, my dear guest. As my brother and I were exactly of the same height, my brother, by way of a joke, sent me a complete Parisian wardrobe, which I was never to wear except on grand occasions, such as when M. the Prefect pays us a visit, when M. the General commanding the eighty-sixth department makes his annual tour, or when we receive a guest like yourself, and have the happiness of coupling that pleasure with the occasion of some solemnity, such as we are about to take part in."

There was a continuous vein of irony running through the conversation of this young man, which, whilst restrained by a superior and well-regulated mind, so as never to trespass beyond the bounds of politeness, was nevertheless calculated to put one ill at ease during a conversation with him. I contented myself, therefore, by inclining my head as a token of thanks, whilst he put on, with all the appropriate precautions, a pair of yellow gloves, made to the hand by Boivin or by Rousseau. Thus accoutred, he had the air of a veritable Parisian. By this time I had finished my toilet, and the clock had struck the three quarters past nine.

"Come," said he, "if you wish to see the show, I think it is about time that we should take our positions: at least, however, if you would not prefer a quiet lunch instead—which to me, I admit, appears the most reasonable."

I thanked him, but assured him I rarely ate before one o'clock in the day, so that I could accomplish the two affairs very easily.

"Come on, then," said he. Taking up my hat, I followed my host.

CHAPTER XI.

FROM the elevation of the ladder of eight steps by which we had attained the door of the castellated mansion inhabited by Madame de Franchi and her son, we looked over the square or open plot of ground in front of the church. This *place* presented an aspect very different from its usual solitary appearance—being now covered by people: but all this crowd was

---

* A celebrated tailor in Paris, the equal in fame of our Stultz.—*Trans.*

composed of females and of children under twelve years of age : not a man was present among them.

Upon the first step of the church-porch stood a solemn-looking personage, with a tri-colour scarf over his shoulder : this was the mayor.

Under the portico, another man dressed in black, was sitting at a table, with some written papers in his hand. This man was the notary. The papers contained the rough sketch of the act of reconciliation.

I took my place at one side of the table, with the Orlandi's witnesses : opposite were the witnesses of the Colona : behind the notary, Lucien stationed himself, as being a spot equally remote from one party as the other. In the body of the church we could see the priests in their vestments, ready to perform mass.

The clock struck ten. As the clock struck a violent surging of the crowd took place ; each one striving to get a sight of the two extremities of the street—if one might so call the irregular interval left between its fifty houses—each house built according to the capricious fancy of its original proprietor.

Immediately after we could see Orlandi approaching the place of meeting from the mountain side ; whilst on the opposite or river side, came Colona : each was accompanied by his partisans : but, in accordance with the programme agreed upon, not one of them carried any arms : indeed, we may say that, leaving out of the question the acerbity or waspish expression of their countenances, they looked like honest churchwardens going to take their part in a parish procession.

The two chiefs of the parties presented, in a physical point of view, a remarkable contrast ; Orlandi, as I have before said, was tall, slender, dark complexioned, and lively. Colona was short, thickset, and strong, his beard and hair were red, and both were cut short and stubbly. Each of them carried an olive branch in one hand, a poetic conceit of the mayor : Colona held by the feet in the other hand a white fowl, destined to replace, by way of damages for property destroyed, the fowl which, ten years before, had given rise to the quarrel. The fowl was alive. I mention this fact because the point was for a long time discussed with great heat, and had threatened more than once to put an end to the affair, as Colona looked on it in the light of a double humiliation to render back a live fowl for the dead one which his aunt had flung into the face of her cousin the Orlandi. However, by sheer strength of logic, Lucien had overcome the scruples of Colona, and by force of style and argument he had induced Orlandi to receive it. At the moment the two enemies appeared, the bells struck out all at once into a merry joy peal.

On first perceiving each other, Orlandi and Colona, by a mutual movement of aversion, showed clearly the reciprocal repulsive action within : however, they each passed on towards the church. Opposite the church door, they both stopped at about four yards distance from each other. Now, three days previously to this, had these men encountered or come within sight at a hundred yards distance from each other, in all probability one of them would never have gone alive from the spot. Thus they stood for five minutes, not only the two distinct groups, but also the whole mass of people—silent and motionless—a silence and inertness which, in spite of the conciliatory purpose for which the assembly was convened, presented anything but a pacific character.

The Mayor now broke the ominous stillness.

"Come, come," said he, "Colona, don't you know that you are to speak first."

Colona, after a terrific internal struggle, spoke some words in the Corsican *patois*. I understood them to express his regret that he should have been at enmity (*vendetta*) with his good neighbour Orlandi for so many years ; and that he had come to offer, as a reparation, the white fowl which he held in his hand.

Orlandi waited until the speech of his adversary was thus neatly concluded, when he responded by some words in the same dialect, which went so far as to promise that he would remember only the reconciliation which had thus taken place under the auspices of the Mayor, by the arbitration of M. Lucien, and in the handwriting of the Notary.

For a second time the two chiefs lapsed into a dead silence.

"Very good ! gentlemen," said the Mayor, "it appears to me that it will be necessary, in the next place, to give the hand of good fellowship to each other."

By an instinctive movement, the two enemies carried their hands behind them.

The Mayor descended from the steps on which he had stood, and first caught the hand of Colona, then that of Orlandi, and after some efforts, the awkwardness of which he essayed to dissipate by a smile, he succeeded in joining their hands.

Then the notary, seizing the lucky moment, rose from his seat, and whilst the Mayor was occupied in holding firmly the hands of the two ex-belligerents, which at the first seemed very much inclined to separate, but which finally resigned themselves to rest placidly one in the other, the notary read as follows :

"Before us, Joseph Antonio Sarrola, notary-royal at Sullacaro, in the province of Sartène, in the Grand Square of the village, opposite the Church, in the presence of Monsieur the Mayor, the witnesses, and all the assembly. BETWEEN Gaetano Orso Orlandi, surnamed Orlandini, and Marco Vicenzo Colona, surnamed Schioppione, the following solemn covenant and agreement has been drawn up :

"From this day, the 4th March, 1841, the *vendetta* existing for the last ten years between the above families shall for ever cease.

"Henceforth and from this day they shall live together as good neighbours and fellow-countrymen, as their forefathers lived before the unhappy affair which gave rise to the disunion and enmity between their families and friends.

"In witness of this, they have each signed these presents, under the porch of the village church, together with M. Polo Arbori, mayor of the commune, M. Lucien de Franchi, arbitrator, the witnesses to the two contracting parties, and ourself, notary.

"Sullacaro, the 4th day of March, 1841."

"But at the porch, at the solicitation of the Mayor, they again joined hands."—*Page* 29.

I could not help admiring the tact and pru-
dence of the notary in having totally abstained
from the remotest allusion to the fowl which
placed Colona in such a humiliating position
before Orlandi.

In proportion as the countenance of Colona
brightened, so inversely did that of Orlandi
become darkened. The last look which he gave
at the fowl, which· was held by one of the men,
evidently evinced a violent temptation to hurl
it into Colona's face. But a glance of the eye
from Lucien de Franchi stopped the base intent
in its bud.

The mayor saw there was no time to be lost;
he mounted the steps backwards, still holding
the two reconciliants by the hands, and keeping
his eyes steadily fixed on them. Then, in order
to prevent any punctilious debate at the moment
of signing, seeing that each one of the two belli-
gerents would have held it as a concession made
to the other if he signed the deed first, he took
the pen and signed the deed first, and, turning
shame into honour, passed the pen to Orlandi,
who signed and passed the pen to Lucien, who,
using the same pacific subterfuge, passed it in
his turn to Colona, who affixed his mark.

At this moment the village church re-echoed
with the voices of the priests as they chanted
the *Te Deum* after the victory.

Every one present signed in their turn, without

"Monsieur, I would not wish you to leave Sullacaro without my thanking you for the honour you have done a poor peasant like myself."—*Page 30.*

regard to rank or title, as the French nobility did, one hundred and twenty-three years before, the protest against the Duke of Maine.

Then the two heroes of the day entered the church, and kneeling down, one on each side of the choir, took part in the religious ordinances. From that moment I could see a perfect tranquillity in the features of Lucien: all was finished, the reconciliation was sworn, not only before men, but before God.

Mass terminated, Orlandi and Colona retired from the church with the same ceremony as on entering it. But at the porch, at the solicitation of the Mayor, they again joined hands, and each one, with his friends and partisans, took the road to his house, into which, for a period of three

years before this, they had not once entered; Lucien and I repaired to Madame Franchi's, where dinner awaited us.

It was easy for me to discover—above all, by the attention he lavished on me—that Lucien had read my name over my shoulder at the time I had subscribed it at the foot of the document; and it was equally certain that the name seemed not totally unknown to him.

On the following morning, I announced to Lucien my intention of setting out on my return to Paris, after dinner; in fact, it was imperatively necessary that I should be present at the rehearsals of *Un Mariage sous Louis XV.*; and, notwithstanding the earnest entreaties of the mother and the son, I persisted in my original intention. Lucien then claimed to make use of my proffered services in conveying a letter to his brother; and Madame de Franchi, who, hidden under her Spartan stoicism, had all the tenderness of a mother's love, made me promise to give the letter to her son with my own hands. The trouble, it may be remarked, was in no ways great, for Louis de Franchi, true Parisian as he was, resided at No. 7, Rue du Helder. I again asked Lucien to allow me to pass in review the various articles before alluded to in his chamber: he conducted me there himself, and having made a close inspection of its various curiosities, he observed: "Understand, now, if there is any one article here you have a fancy for, take it—it is your own." I detached a small poignard from its place in an obscure corner which indicated that it was of no great value, and, as I had seen Lucien look with some degree of curiosity at my hunting-belt, and had sometimes admired its arrangement, I begged him to accept it. He had the good taste to take it, without giving me the pain of twice urging. At this juncture, Griffo appeared at the door, and announced that the horse was saddled, and that the guide was waiting.

I had put on one side the present I intended to make to Griffo: it was a sort of hunting-knife, with two small pistols, one on each side of the blade, and of which the locks were hidden in the handle. I never saw joy so manifest and exuberant as he evinced on obtaining possession of this article.

On descending from my chamber I found Madame de Franchi at the foot of the staircase. On the same spot from which she had welcomed me to her house, she again stood to wish me a pleasant voyage. I lifted her hands to my lips: indeed, I felt a great respect for this woman—in whom, simplicity was so mixed with dignity.

At the door, to which I was conducted by Lucien, he observed: "On any other occasion, I should have saddled my horse, and gone with you from hence to the mountain: but to day, I dare not quit Sullacaro, for fear that one or the other of our newly-made friends should commit themselves by some silly action."

"You will act wisely in so doing," said I. "As for myself, I believe I have cause to felicitate myself on having been an eye-witness to a ceremony in Corsica, so rare and remarkable as that in which I have taken a part."

"True—true," said he, "you may consider yourself fortunate ; for you have been witness to that which ought to have made our forefathers start up from their graves."

"I can well understand that. In their days their bare word would have been held sufficiently sacred to have rendered unnecessary the intervention of a notary or of witnesses."

"They would never have been reconciled at all."

He held out his hand to me.

"Will you not charge me with an embrace for your brother ?" asked I.

"Doubtless: if it would not be inconvenient to you."

"Let us embrace, my friend. I can never sufficiently thank you for the kindness I have experienced from you."

"Shall I not have the pleasure of again seeing you some day ?" asked I.

"Yes : that is, if you return to Corsica."

"No—say rather, when you come to Paris," said I.

"That I shall never do."

"At all events, if you should, you will find my card on your brother's mantel-piece. Don't forget the address."

"I promise you, that if any extraordinary event should call me on the Continent, to you will my first visit be paid."

"So—that is agreed on."

He held out his hand for a parting shake, and we parted. He followed me with his eyes as I descended the street which led to the river.

The village seemed tranquil enough, but there was still that sort of groundswell of agitation which is always the resultant of some previous great event. I cast my eyes from door to door, as I passed down the street, making sure that I should see my friend Orlandi, and that he might come out to thank me for my having acted godfather on the late occasion. But I looked in vain : I reached the last house in the village, and stepped forth into the open country without seeing anything of him. I believe I had wellnigh forgotten the affair altogether,—and I may here add, that when I reflected on the grave and weighty affair which Orlandi had had to take part in or carry out, I did not wonder at his forgetfulness—when all at once, on arriving at Bicchisano, I saw, emerging from the thicket, a man, who placed himself in the middle of the path : a moment's glance shewed me it was the very same individual, who, in my French impatience, and my Parisian notions of the observances of society, I had taxed with ingratitude. I observed that he had donned the same habiliments that he wore on the occasion of his interview with Lucien in the ruins of Vicentello —he carried his cartouche-box, to which was attached his pistol, and he was armed with a rifle. When he was twenty yards from me, he saluted me by putting his hand to his hat ; whilst I, on my part, put the spur to my horse that I should not keep him waiting.

"Monsieur," said he to me, "I would not wish you to leave Sullacaro without my thanking you for the honour you have done a poor peasant like myself in having appeared as his guarantee, and, as in the village below I had neither my heart at ease nor my tongue free, I am come here to see you."

"I thank you," said I, "but there was no necessity for you to put yourself out of the way for this : the honour is for me."

"You see," continued the bandit, "we cannot lose the habit of forty years in one moment. The mountain air is strong: after once being accustomed to respire it, we are suffocated in any other atmosphere. In those miserable houses, I am every moment expecting the roof to fall upon my head."

"But," replied I, "you can now go back to your regular mode of life. You have a house, they tell me, fields, and vineyard."

"Undoubtedly ; but my sister keeps the house, and the Lucquois are there to till the fields and sell the grapes. Corsicans, such as I am, never work."

"How do you pass your time then?"

"We overlook those who do work, we walk about with our guns on our shoulders, we hunt."

"Ah, good! my dear Orlandi," said I to him, giving him my hand, "very fine hunting. But recollect that my honour, as well as your own is engaged thus far, that you will never fire a gun except to shoot the mouflon, the buck, the boar, the pheasant, or the partridge: never again are you to draw trigger against Marco Vicenzio Colona or any of his family."

"Ah! Excellence," replied my godson, with an expression of physiognomy which I never remarked except upon the countenance of a Norman pleader, "the fowl he gave back to us was a very lean one."

And, without adding another word, he plunged into the thicket, and disappeared. I continued on my way, meditating upon this probable cause of a new rupture between the Orlandi and the Colona.

That same evening I slept at Albiteccia. The next day I reached Ajaccio; and eight hours afterwards I was in Paris.

PART II.

CHAPTER XII.

On the same day that I arrived in Paris, I presented myself at the residence of Monsieur Louis de Franchi: he was from home. I left my card and a note, stating that I had come direct from Sullacaro, and that I had in my charge a letter from M. Lucien, his brother. I asked of him to name his hour, and added that I had engaged to deliver the letter to him personally.

In conducting me to the library of his master, in order to write my note, the servant led me successively through the saloon and dining-room. I marked with a curious eye the various objects I passed on my way, and I recognised the same taste which I had seen displayed at Sullacaro—only with this difference, that it was heightened and refined by Parisian elegance. M. Louis de Franchi had indeed a very charming bachelor residence.

The day following, as I was dressing—it might be about one o'clock—my servant announced M. de Franchi. I gave orders that he should be led into the saloon, that the day's papers should be given to him, and a message with it that I would wait on him in a few minutes. In fact, in less than five I entered the saloon. Aroused by the noise I made, M. de Franchi, who had begun reading—led by politeness, no doubt—a *feuilleton* of my own, which at that time I was engaged on for *La Presse*, raised his head. I stopped, perfectly astounded at his resemblance to his brother.

"Monsieur," said he, rising from his seat, "I could hardly believe in my good fortune on reading the note which you left at my place yesterday. I have made my valet repeat five several times his description of you in order to assure myself that it corresponded with your well-known portrait. In short, in my twofold impatience to thank you and to obtain intelligence from my dear mother and brother, I have presented myself here without any knowledge as to your hours of reception, and, in truth, I fear I have made too early a call on you."

"Pardon me, if I do not reply at first to your flattering compliment: but I confess to you, Monsieur, that, looking at you, I am obliged to ask myself the question, Is it Monsieur Louis or Monsieur Lucien de Franchi I am addressing?"

"Yes; the resemblance is indeed great, is it not?" added he, smiling; "and even when I was at Sullacaro, there were few there whom we could not deceive. However, if he has not, since my departure, renounced his Corsican habits, you must have seen him in a costume which would present some difference."

"As accident would have it," I rejoined, "when I quitted your brother's house, he was dressed, with the exception that he wore white pantaloons, exactly as you are now; consequently, on my first seeing you, I had not that difference of costume of which you speak in my mind. But,' said I, taking the letter from my portmanteau, "I can sufficiently comprehend your anxiety to hear news from your relatives. Here is the letter; I would have sent it to you yesterday, if I had not promised Madame de Franchi to give it you personally."

"Were they all well when you left them?"

"Yes; but rather anxious."

"About me?"

"Yes. But I pray you, read your letter."

"With your permission?"

M. de Franchi broke the seal, while I occupied myself in making some cigarettes. As he proceeded through the letter he smiled, and at intervals muttering, "Dear Lucien!" "My loving mother!" "I can well understand that!" and it was thus whilst looking at him, I could not avoid being struck by the exact resemblance to his brother in Corsica; though, as Lucien had stated, a very close scrutiny informed me that his countenance was of a pale cast: there was also a difference in their respective pronunciation of French—Louis speaking it like a true Parisian.

"Well," said I, as I handed him a cigarette, after he had finished reading the letter, "you have read, as I told you was the case, that your family were in some anxiety on your account: but I am happy to see that they were wrong."

"No;" said he to me, sorrowfully: "not at all wrong. It is true, I have not been in ill-health; but I have been in much trouble, which, I must

SOTAIN

"I stopped, perfectly astounded at his resemblance to his brother."—*Page* 31.

confess, has been greatly augmented by the knowledge of the uneasiness it must have cost my dear brother."

"Monsieur Lucien has already informed me of the peculiar circumstances you allude to," I replied; "but in good truth, did I not believe that so extraordinary a phenomenon was a truth, and not merely the result of a peculiarity of idea, I should require no more proof than I receive at this moment; and, indeed you yourself are convinced, sir, that the unhappiness experienced by your brother at Corsica is the result of the trouble you have fallen into here?"

"Yes. Of that I am perfectly convinced!"

"In that case," replied I, "as your answer in the affirmative has doubled the interest I have

before felt in your affairs, allow me to ask you, as a friend and not from idle curiosity, if the cause of the uneasiness you have had is passed, or if you have any means of alleviating or removing it?"

"Oh, my God! you know sir," said he, "that time will dull the most acute sorrow; and if the heart's wound be not envenomed, though it may bleed at times, still it will in time cicatrize, though it leave a scar. But, however this may be, again I beg you to receive my warmest thanks, and let me hope that I may obtain permission occasionally to give you a look in, and chat about Sullacaro."

"To me it will be a great pleasure; but why," said I, "not continue at the present moment a

"A mask, with a bouquet of myosotis in one hand, and who had perhaps heard the last portion of our conversation, took the arm of D—— and led him off."—*Page* 34.

conversation which is so agreeable. Listen : here is my servant come to announce that luncheon is on the table. Do me then the favour of discussing a chop with me, and then we can chat at our ease."

"I am sorry that it is impossible. I received yesterday a letter from the keeper of the seals, praying me to go at noon to the office of the Minister of Justice ; and you will easily understand that I, a poor little advocate at grass, must not let so important a law officer wait for me."

"Ah ! probably he wishes to consult you respecting the affair of the Orlandi and the Colona."

"I presume it is ; and, as my brother writes me that the quarrel is terminated"—

"In presence of a notary—I give it you as a positive fact, seeing that I signed the contract, in the capacity of Orlandi's surety."

"So my brother informs me. Now," added he, looking at his watch, "it wants a few minutes of twelve o'clock : I shall go first to announce to the keeper of the seals that my brother has freed me from my engagement."

"That he has religiously kept your guarantee I can indeed vouch."

"Dear Lucien ! I know well, whatever his own sentiments, he would do so."

"He did it, as if of his own good will and inclination, though I know what it must have cost him in his own mind."

"We shall talk of this again at some future

time. Indeed you can well appreciate the fact that it is a great happiness for me to review, in my mind's eye, the pictures recalled by your visit—of my mother, my brother, and my country. So, if you will name your time"—

"That would be rather difficult now. During the first few days after my return I shall be rather in the vagrant way. But tell me where I shall find you."

"Listen !" said he to me, "to-morrow is Mid-Lent, is it not ?"

"To-morrow ?"

"Yes."

"Well—what of that ?"

"Shall you be at the opera ball ?"

"Yes—and no. Yes: if you ask me to give you a rendezvous: no; that is I have no other business to call me there."

"It is absolutely imperative on me: I am obliged to be there."

"Oh, oh !" said I, smiling, "I see very clearly, as you just observed, that time deadens the most poignant griefs, and that the wounded heart will eventually heal."

"You are completely at fault: for in all probability, I go to seek a fresh agony."

"Then why go ?"

"Ah ! my God ! can we do what we wish in this world. I am forced there in spite of myself: I go wherever impelled by an irresistible fatality. Far better were it for me if I did not —that I know well—nevertheless, I go."

"To-morrow, at the opera, be it then ?"

"Yes."

"At what time ?"

"At half-past twelve—if it will suit you."

"In what part of the house ?"

"In the pit. At one o'clock—I shall expect you before that."

"Agreed."

We shook hands, and he hurriedly left.

I occupied myself during the remainder of that and the whole of the following day, in those matters and arrangements which are indispensably necessary after a return from an eighteen months' voyage. At half-past twelve in the evening I repaired to the place of meeting. Louis had been there for some time previous. He had followed into the corridors a mask which he thought he had recognised, but he had lost sight of her amidst the crowd.

I was about to speak to him of Corsica, but Louis seemed too pre-occupied to follow so grave a subject; his eyes being constantly directed to the timepiece. On a sudden he left me, exclaiming—

"Ah ! I see the bouquet of violets." So saying, he elbowed his way through the crowd, in order to reach a lady, who held in her hand an enormous bouquet of violets."

As, luckily for the promenaders, there were in the pit bouquets of every sort, I was immediately accosted by the bearer of a bouquet of camelias, who congratulated me on my return to Paris. To the camelias succeeded rosebuds; after the rosebuds followed the sunflower; and in this manner, I had reached my fifth congratulation and bouquet, when I encountered D——

"Ah ! is it you, my dear fellow," said he—"welcome home—you have arrived just in the

nick of time. We intend supping to-night with three or four friends of ours, and of course we shall reckon on you."

"I thank you a thousand times, my good friend," answered I, "but in spite of my ardent wish to accept your invitation, I cannot do it, since I have some one with me."

"But I can't see why you cannot understand that every one has a right to bring his friend. It is perfectly understood that there will be six flower-vases on the table, destined to receive the ladies' bouquets, and to keep them fresh."

"Ah, my dear friend, you are all wrong: I shall bring no bouquet to put in your vases—my friend is a male."

"Well, what then, you know the proverb, 'Love me, love my friend.'"

"He is a young man whom you do not know."

"Good—then we shall make his acquaintance."

"I will tell him of his good luck."

"Yes, and if he refuses—make him come."

"I will promise you to do all I can : but at what hour do you sup ?"

"At three—and continue open till six : so you have a wide margin."

"Very good."

A mask, with a bouquet of myosotis in one hand, and who had perhaps heard the last portion of our conversation, took the arm of D—— and led him off.

A few moments after this, I again met Louis, who, it seemed had finished his interview with the lady carrying the bouquet of violets.

As my domino was endowed with but a very mediocre style of wit, I sent her on an embassy to puzzle one of my friends, and took the arm of Louis.

"Well," said I to him, "have you learnt all you wished to know ?"

"Ah ! you know well enough that we hear things spoken at a masked ball of which we had better have remained in ignorance."

"My poor friend !" said I to him. "Excuse my calling you so : but it really appears to me that I know you as well as your brother. You are unhappy, are you not ? What is it, then, that annoys you ?"

"Oh—it is nothing worth the trouble of repeating."

I saw that he wished to keep his secret, and I desisted. We made two or three turns round the ball-room in silence : I was indifferent enough to the scene, but my companion's eyes were eternally on the watch, scrutinising every domino as it passed by the door out of our sight.

"Now !" said I to him, "What do you intend to do ?"

He was startled, as if suddenly interrupted in a deep train of thought.

"I—no ! What do you say—I beg pardon."

"I wish to propose to you a change of scene, which I think would do you no harm."

"What is it ?"

"Come and sup with me at a friend's house ?"

"Oh, no ! I should make but a dull companion."

"Pshaw ! Let's talk of amusement: we shall be jolly there."

"Besides—I am not invited."

"There you are wrong : you are invited."

"That's very kind of your Amphitryon; but, on my honour I do not feel worthy"—

At that moment we came across D——, who appeared very deeply engaged with the mask with the bouquet of myosotis. He saw me, notwithstanding.

"Ah! good!" said he, "is it convenient? Will you and your friend come?"

"Less convenient than ever, my dear fellow: I cannot sup with you to-night."

"Go to the devil, then!" he exclaimed in a pet, going off with the lady.

"Who is that gentleman?" asked Louis of me, merely for the sake of breaking the silence.

"That is D——, one of our friends; a man of great wit, and manager of one of our leading journals."

"Monsieur D——! Monsieur D——!" exclaimed Louis. "Do you know him well?"

"Intimately. I have been engaged the last two or three years in a business way with him: and more than that, we are on terms of friendship."

"Is it at his house that you intended supping?"

"Yes."

"That alters the case: I accept your invitation—oh, yes. I accept it with great pleasure."

"So much the better."

"Perhaps I ought not to go," replied Louis, anxiously: "but you recollect what I told you yesterday: we do not always go where we ought, but where destiny forces us: and for proof of this, it would be much better for me not to go to-night with you; yet I shall go."

At this time we again encountered D——.

"My dear friend," said I, "I have changed my mind."

"Then you will be with us?"

"Yes."

"Bravo. Meanwhile I ought to tell you one thing."

"What is that?"

"It is that every one supping with us to-night must do the same to-morrow night."

"By virtue of what law?"

"By virtue of a wager made with Chateau-Renaud."

I felt Louis tremble violently, as his arm was resting on mine. This made me turn round; I saw that, though paler than usual, no other trace of emotion was visible in his features."

"And what is this bet?" asked I of D——.

"Oh, it would take up too much time to tell you all about it here. Besides, there is a lady interested in this affair, and if she were to hear aught of it, the bet would most likely be lost."

"Indeed! Well, at three o'clock I shall see you."

"At three."

We separated: and on looking at the time-piece, I found it was half past two.

"Do you know this Monsieur de Chateau-Renaud?" asked Louis, in a voice in which he vainly tried to hide the emotion he felt.

"By sight only: I have met him sometimes in society."

"Then he is not a friend of yours?"

"He is simply an acquaintance."

"Ah! so much the better," said Louis.

"Why?"

"Nothing."

"But it would seem you know him yourself?"

"Indirectly I do."

Notwithstanding the evasive character of the answer, it was easy for me to discover that there was between M. de Franchi and M. de Chateau-Renaud, one of those mysterious relations of which a woman is sure to be the connecting link. An instinctive apprehension of some undefined evil compelled me to believe that it would be much better for my companion if he never entered the house.

"One moment, Monsieur de Franchi," said I, "will you take my advice."

"In what particular?"

"Don't go to the supper at D——'s."

"For what reason. They will be waiting for us; and what is more, you have told them you would bring a friend with you."

"Very true: but that is not the reason."

"Then, what is?"

"Simply, because I believe that it will be all the better if we do not go."

"But you certainly must have some reason for changing your mind; up to this moment you insisted on my going, almost against my own will."

"We shall be sure to meet with M. de Chateau-Renaud."

"So much the better. He is a very amiable personage; and I shall be delighted in obtaining a more intimate knowledge of him."

"Well—be it as you like. Let us go, since you will have it so."

We immediately went into the lower rooms for our paletots. D—— dwelt at some distance from the opera: as it was a fine night, and I was of opinion that a walk in the open air would calm my friend's perturbation, I proposed it to him: he consented.

CHAPTER XIII.

On reaching the saloon, we found there several of my friends—frequenters of the pit, or occasional loungers in the slips at the opera. With these were some two or three unmasked dominoes, holding in their hands enormous bouquets of rich flowers, about to plant them in the vases on the table. I introduced M. Louis de Franchi to the company: it is needless to say the introduction was welcomed.

Shortly after, D—— entered the room, accompanied by the lady with the bouquet of myosotis. She unmasked with a facility and *abandon* which, while it showed her to possess exquisite beauty of features, gave as evident indications of a lady to whom such parties were far from being unusual.

I presented M. de Franchi to D——.

"Now," said B—— "if all the introductions are made, let us seat ourselves at table."

"The introductions are made, but all our guests are not here," said D——.

"Who is the absent one?"

"Chateau-Renaud is not here."

"Oh—you're right. Is there not a bet with him," asked V——.

M. de Chateau-Renaud.—*Page* 35.

"Yes, a wager for a supper for twelve, that he brings with him a certain lady."

"And who may this lady be," asked the lady with the bouquet of myosotis, "who is so rigidly virtuous, that she must be made the subject of such a wager."

"I'faith," responded D—— to the last speaker, "I don't believe there can be a very great indiscretion committed in naming the lady—the more so, as in all probability none of you are acquainted with her.   It is Madame"——

Louis put his hand on D——'s arm. "Sir," said he, "on the strength of our new acquaintance, I have to request a favour of you?"

"What is it, sir?"

"Forbear to name the person who is to accompany M. de Chateau-Renaud: you know she is a married woman."

"Yes: but then her husband is at Smyrna, in the East Indies, at Mexico—or I don't know where.   When a husband is at such a respectable distance, you know, it is very much the same thing to the wife as if she was unmarried."

"Her husband will one day return: I know him well: he is a brave and a good man, and I should wish, if possible, to spare him the annoyance of learning, on return, that his wife had done a thing so inconsistent."

"Then, sir, I beg your pardon," said D——. "I was not aware that you knew anything of the lady: I was in doubt whether she was a married woman or single; but, since you are acquainted with her—since you know her husband"——

" 'To their health !' said D——."—Page 38.

"I know them well."

"In that case, we shall certainly keep ourselves within the strictest bounds of discretion. Ladies and gentlemen,— whether Chateau-Renaud comes or not—whether he comes alone or with others—whether he loses or gains his wager, I must ask of you the favour to keep the whole of the adventure secret."

Profound secresy was unanimously promised; this readiness to oblige probably not being so much owing to respect for the conventionalities of society, as it arose from the guests being rather hungry, and, by a natural consequence, very anxious to begin supper.

"I thank you, sir," said de Franchi to D——, giving him his hand. "I was sure that you would act like a man of honour."

We immediately repaired from the saloon to the *salle-à-manger*, where each one took his seat. Two seats remained unoccupied: they were intended for Chateau-Renaud and the lady he was engaged, under forfeiture, to bring with him. The waiter was about to lift the dish-covers, when he was stopped by our host, saying—

"No: let it be. Chateau-Renaud has another quarter of an hour. In a quarter of an hour's time you may lift the covers: when the time-piece strikes three-quarters, the wager will be decided."

I did not lose sight of M. de Franchi, but saw him turn his eyes towards the mantel-piece: the index of the time-piece marked twenty minutes to four.

"Is it correct?" he asked coldly.

"That's no affair of mine," said D——, laughing, "that is Chateau-Renaud's business. I regulated the time-piece by his watch, in order that he should have no reason to say that I took him by surprise."

"Eh, gentlemen," said the lady with the bouquet of myosotis, " since we may not talk of Chateau-Renaud and his unknown, let us change the subject, else we shall be talking riddles and enigmas, which, by-the-bye, is mortal tiresome."

"You are quite right," observed V—— "there are many ladies of whom we may speak, and who desire nothing better than that they may be talked about."

"To their health," said D——. And each of our companions filled his glass from the bottle of iced champagne close to his hand and drank the toast. Louis, however, barely touched his lips with the glass.

"Drink, my friend," said I to him: "you can perceive clearly that she will not be here."

"There is still some time to elapse: let the quarter-hour arrive, and I promise you to drink with the best of them."

"We shall see."

Whilst we exchanged those few words in a low voice, the conversation become general and noisy; Louis, from time to time reverted his eyes to the time-piece, which moved on in dull unvaried impassibility, despite the anxiety of the two persons who so frequently consulted its index. It was within five minutes of the decisive moment: turning to Louis, I said, "Your health!" He took up his glass, smiled, and carried it to his lips, but had scarce half emptied it ere the sound of the bell struck on our ears. I had believed that no man could be paler than Louis ordinarily was: I was deceived.

"It is him!" he cried.

"Possibly: but perhaps it may not be her," answered I.

"A moment more, and we shall see."

The sound of the bell had aroused the attention of every one; this was indicated by the profound silence which succeeded the noisy and laughing conversation before alluded to.

We heard a noise of some persons discussing or talking earnestly in the antechamber.

D—— immediately rose and went to open the door.

"It is—it is her voice!" said Louis, seizing me by the wrist, which he grasped with considerable force.

"Come, come, courage! be a man," I replied. "It is very evident that if she comes here to sup at the house of a man with whom she has no acquaintance, and with men who know as little of her, she is a mere wanton, and a woman of that class is unworthy of the love of a man of honour."

"But I beg of you to come in, madame," said D——, "I assure you, you will only be among friends."

"Do come in, my dear Emilie," said M. de Chateau-Renaud, "you need not unmask if you do not wish to do so."

"Wretch!" murmured Louis de Franchi.

As he spoke, a lady entered, dragged rather than conducted into the room by D—— and Chateau-Renaud, the former believing himself bound to do his *devoirs* as master of the house.

"Won, by three minutes!" said Chateau-Renaud in a low voice to D——.

"Good, my dear fellow, you've won."

"Not yet, sir," said the young unknown visitress, addressing herself to Chateau-Renaud, and drawing herself up to her full height, " for I now understand the reason of your perseverance—you have made a bet that you would bring me here to supper, have you not?"

Chateau-Renaud was silent. She then turned to D——.

"Since this man refuses to answer my question, answer it yourself," said she. "Is it not the fact that M. de Chateau-Renaud has laid a wager that he would bring me to sup with you?"

"I cannot disguise from you, madame, that M. de Chateau-Renaud has flattered me with this hope."

"Very good. M. de Chateau-Renaud has lost his wager; for I was ignorant as to where I was to be conducted, believing it to be to a friend's house: and, as I did not come here voluntarily, it appears to me to be very evident that M. de Chateau-Renaud ought, in all fairness, to lose the wager."

"But, now that you are here, dear Emilie," again intreated M. de Chateau-Renaud, "you will remain—will you not? See, you will have a goodly company of gentlemen, and a joyous company of ladies."

"Now that I am here," said the unknown lady, "I must thank you, sir, who appear to be the master of the house, for the kind manner in which you have welcomed me: but, as unfortunately I cannot respond to so gracious an invitation, I would beg M. Louis de Franchi to give me his arm and conduct me to my home."

Louis made but one bound from his seat, and found himself in one second standing between the lady and M. de Chateau-Renaud.

"I would beg to observe, madame," said the latter, through his teeth, set with rage, "that I am the person who brought you here—it is for me to conduct you back."

"Gentlemen," said the unknown, "you are here—five men. I put myself under the safeguard of your honour; I trust you will not allow M. de Chateau-Renaud to do me a violence."

Chateau-Renaud made a movement towards her: we all rose from our seats.

"It is well, madame, you are free; I know what remains for me to do."

"If that is for me, sir," said Louis de Franchi, with an air of fierce disdain impossible to depict in words, "you will always find me at No. 7, rue du Helder."

"Very good, perhaps I may not have the honour of presenting myself to you personally, but I hope in my stead and on my behalf you will receive two of my friends."

"You are forgetting yourself, sir," said Louis de Franchi, shrugging his shoulders, " in talking of such an affair in a lady's presence. Come, madame," continued he, placing the arm of the unknown lady within his, " and believe that from the very depths of my soul I thank you for the honour you have done me."

They both retired amid a silence almost painful.

"Ah! well, what of it, gentlemen?" said Chateau-Renaud, when the door was shut, "I have lost the wager—that's clear. To-morrow night every one here will sup at the 'Brothers of Provence.'"

So saying, he sat down in one of the vacant seats, and held out his glass to D——, who filled it to the brim.

However, as may perhaps be surmised, in spite of the noisy hilarity of M. de Chateau-Renaud, the supper passed off very flatly.

CHAPTER XIV.

On the morrow—I ought rather to have said the same day at ten o'clock in the morning, I was at the door of M. Louis de Franchi's residence. Going up stairs I met two young men coming down: one of them was evidently a man about town—or as the phrase goes, "a man of the world," the other, wearing the medal of the Legion of Honor on his coat, though dressed as a civilian, I felt sure was a military man. I had my doubts as to whether these two men had not come from M. de Franchi's apartments; after following them with my eyes to the foot of the staircase, I went on my way, and rung the bell. The servant opened, and informed me that his master was in his study. As he entered to announce me, Louis turned his head.

"Oh! the very man!" exclaimed he, tearing up a note he had been engaged in writing, and throwing its fragments into the grate, "this note was for you—I was about to send it. Now, Joseph, I am not at home to any one."

Joseph retired.

"Did you not meet two gentlemen on the stairs?" asked Louis, handing me a chair.

"Yes: one of them with the cross of the Legion of Honour."

"The very same."

"I fancied they came from your apartments."

"You were right in your conjecture."

"Did they not come on the part of M. Chateau-Renaud?"

"They are his seconds."

"The devil! has this affair taken so serious a turn as that?"

"It could take no other; you must agree with me there," replied Louis.

"And they came"—

"To ask me to send two friends to talk over the preliminaries. It was then that I thought of you."

"I am much honored by your remembrance, but I can do nothing by myself."

"I have asked one of my friends, the Baron Giordano Martelli, to lunch with me. We shall all three lunch together, and at noon you will be good enough to go with him to the residences of those gentlemen, who have promised to be at home until three o'clock. Here are their names and addresses." So saying, he put two cards into my hand. The one was that of the Baron Réné de Chateaugrand, the other, M. Adrien de Boissy. The first-named resided at No. 12, Rue la Paix;

the second, as I had premised, was an officer in the army—a lieutenant in the African chasseurs, and resided at No. 29, Rue de Lille. I turned and returned the cards about in my hands.

"Well! what annoys you—why are you embarrassed?" asked Louis.

"I wish you to tell me frankly if you think this affair serious. You understand that our operations will be entirely regulated by that fact."

"How!—why serious? You yourself, as well as others, heard what passed: I am challenged by M. de Chateau-Renaud; he has sent his seconds to me. I can do no other than let the affair take its course."

"Yes—very true—but"—

"It is settled then!" replied he, smiling.

"But still I wish to know the cause of the quarrel. We do not stand by and see men cut each other's throats without at least having some knowledge of the origin of the fight. You know that the position of a second is even more responsible than that of principal in a duel."

"Well, I will tell you in a very few words the history of this quarrel. Here you have it. On my arrival in Paris from Corsica, a friend of mine, captain of a frigate in the royal navy, introduced me to his wife. She was pretty—she was young: the first sight of her produced such a deep impression on my feelings, that fearing I should become enamoured of my friend's wife, I profited as rarely as possible by the permission he had given me to make his house my own at any time during my stay in Paris. My friend complained of my indifference, when I frankly confessed to him that his wife was too lovely a woman for me to trust myself to be often in company with. He smiled, gave me his hand, and made me promise that I would dine with him that same day. 'My dear Louis,' he said to me, as we sat over our wine, 'in three weeks' time I shall start for Mexico: I may probably remain there three months: perhaps six—perhaps even longer. We sailors know very exactly the time for sailing—but never that of our return. I confide Emilie to your care during my absence. Emilie, I beg you to receive Louis de Franchi as a brother.'

"The young lady responded to this appeal, and gave me her hand:

"I was thunderstruck: I knew not what answer to make: and I doubtless appeared rather silly in the eyes of my future sister. Well, three months after this conversation, my friend sailed: but during the whole of the three months he remained in France, he had exacted from me a promise that I should dine with him at least once a week. Emilie remained with her mother: I need not say that the confidence reposed in me by the husband rendered the wife sacred: and that, though I loved her with far more than a brother's love, I never looked upon her but with the eyes of a brother. Six months elapsed. During this time Emilie still remained with her mother: I should have added that my friend had strictly enjoined that I should be received at this house. My poor friend feared nothing so much as the reputation of being a jealous man. In fact, he loved his wife to madness, and his confidence in her faith was unbounded. Consequently, I was a not un-

"It is well, madame, you are free; I know what remains for me to do."—*Page* 38.

frequent guest. There were other friends also equally intimate, but the presence of her mother closed the lips of the most malicious scandal-mongers—and left them not even a pretext for censure: up to this time not a breath had ever assailed her reputation as a wife.

"Three months after this M. de Chateau-Renaud was introduced.

"You believe in presentiments, do you not? I shuddered when I first saw him: he did not speak a word to me: he was there in that saloon present only as a man of the world; and, notwithstanding, before he left the room, I felt that I hated him. Wherefore! I cannot say. But how much more was that feeling increased when I saw that the impression which had struck me at first sight of Emilie had also been experienced by himself. It appeared to me that Emilie had treated him with an unaccustomed coquetry; perhaps—nay probably I was deceived; but as I was myself deeply in love with Emilie, I was jealous. Consequently, at the next meeting, I took care to keep my eye on M. de Chateau-Renaud: perhaps he saw through my affectation of not looking at him, whilst my eyes followed him, and it struck me that he talked of me in a low voice to Emilie, and attempted to make me ridiculous. If I had not listened to my better sense, on that night I should have sought a quarrel with him, and have fought with him; but I constrained my feelings on a reflection at the absurdity I was about to

Emilie.—*Page* 39.

commit. From that time, every succeeding Friday was for me a day of torment. M. de Chateau-Renaud was altogether a man of the world, a member of the *bon-ton*, a lion: I could acknowledge in these respects his superiority over me: but it struck me that Emilie elevated him far above his merits. Soon it was made known to me that I was not the only person to perceive the marked preference which Emilie shewed for M. de Chateau-Renaud: indeed this attachment became at last so visible, that one day Giordano, who like me, had the *entrée* to Madame's house, spoke to me of it. From that moment, my decision was taken. I resolved to speak privately to Emilie on the subject, convinced within myself that on her part nothing of consequence had occurred, and that I had only to open her eyes to her own conduct to effect a reformation of that which could only be called lightness of carriage. But, to my great atonishment as well as chagrin, Emilie made a jest of my observations, telling me that I was extremely silly: and that those who thought as I did were as silly as myself. I was firm, and persisted in my remonstrances. She then told me that she would not be judged by me in such an affair, and that a man in love himself was necessarily prejudiced beforehand. I was astounded; her husband, it was evident, had revealed to her all I had confessed to himself. From that time, you will easily perceive that my part, viewed in the light of an unhappy and jealous lover, became a ridiculous one; and consequently, odious to myself. I therefore ceased visiting at Emilie's residence. But although I had desisted from being present at Emilie's parties, I could not avoid hearing of her—of her actions; and I was not a whit less unhappy, because every one had remarked on the assiduities of M. de Chateau-Renaud to Emilie, and it was now common talk. I resolved to write to her. I did so, as cautiously as I possibly could. I begged her, in the name of her wounded honour, in the name of her absent husband, whose confidence in her was unlimited, to watch closely her own conduct. To this I received no answer. What was the event? Love is independent of the will: the poor creature loved,—and loving, she was blind to all things else, or wished to be so. Shortly afterwards, it was the common talk that Emilie was M. de Chateau-Renaud's mistress. I cannot tell you what I felt: but it was at that period that my brother felt the counterpart of the anguish that afflicted my heart. However, a fortnight elapsed after this fact had reached my ears, and meanwhile you arrived in Paris. On the same day that you came to see me, I had received an anonymous letter. This letter, which came from a lady who was unknown to me, appointed a rendezvous at the opera ball: and was to the purport that she had some revelations to make to me relative to the lady of a friend of mine, whom the writer would only indicate at the present time by her Christian name: it was Emilie. I was to recognize my fair correspondent at the ball by her carrying a bouquet of violets. I told you at the time that I should have done better if I had not gone to that place: and I repeat it to you, that I was forced by a fatality to go there.

"Well, I went: I found my domino at the time and place indicated in her note. She confirmed in every paticular all that I had heard relative to M. de Chateau-Renaud having become the favoured lover of Emilie; and as I doubted, or rather seemed to have some doubts of the fact, she gave me this proof, that M. de Chateau-Renaud had laid a wager that he would produce his new mistress at the supper-table of M. D——. It so happened that you were intimate with M. D——; he invited you to the supper; you had liberty to take a friend; you proposed to take me —I accepted; and you know the rest.

"Now, what could I do under these circumstances, but await and accept the challenge now sent me?"

I had nothing to reply to this, so I merely bowed in acquiescence.

"But," I said, after a moment's pause, "I recollect—I trust, however, I have made a mistake—I recollect your brother telling me that you have never in your life handled sword or pistol."

"It is true."

"Then you will be entirely at your adversary's mercy."

"What of it? God will provide."

CHAPTER XV.

As he finished speaking, the valet announced the Baron Giordano Martelli. The Baron was also a Corsican and a native of the province

of Sartène; he served in the 11th regiment, of which corps two or three gallant affairs had made him a captain at the early age of twenty-three: I might add that on the present occasion he was not in military costume.

"Well, well!" said he to Louis, after bowing to me, "the affair has at last come to its proper bearing, and from what thou hast said in thy note, in all probability thou wilt be visited by M. de Chateau-Renaud's seconds."

"They have been here," said Louis.

"And have left their names and addresses?"

"There are their cards."

"Good! thy valet told me lunch was waiting: let us have it up, and we will afterwards return the gentlemens' visit."

We adjourned to the dining-room, and the subject of our previous discussion was dropped. Louis asked me the particulars of my sojourn in Corsica, and I embraced the only opportunity I had of recounting all that I have related. At this moment, when the mind of this young man was calmed by the assurance that he should meet his adversary on the morrow, his thoughts reverted to his country and his family. He made me repeat several times the observations of his brother and his mother to me. He was greatly moved, knowing as he did the true Corsican predilections of his brother, when I detailed to him the care and trouble Lucien had taken to appease the quarrels of the two factions of the Colona and Orsini.

At this moment the clock struck twelve. "I think, gentlemen, without hurrying you in the least," said Louis, "it is high time you returned the visit of those gentlemen: a longer delay might possibly incur a suspicion of neglect on our part."

"Oh! as to that, you may rest yourself contented," replied I, "it is scarcely two hours since they went from here, and we must give them the time to reach their home before our arrival."

"No matter for that," said the Baron, "Louis is in the right."

"Meanwhile," said I, "it is now time for us to know whether you prefer to fight with the sword or the pistol."

"Oh, my God! I have told you it is exactly the same thing to me, seeing that I am unacquainted equally with the one as with the other. Besides, M. de Chateau-Renaud has spared me the embarrassment of choosing. He doubtless looks upon himself as being the party aggrieved, and assuming this, he can choose whatever weapon he pleases."

"However, the offence itself is questionable; you have done nothing more than give your arm to a lady who demanded it."

"Listen to me," said Louis to me in reply, "any discussion, in my opinion, could only take the colouring of a wish to arrange the affair. I am of a peaceable turn of mind, as you are aware; I cannot be charged with being a lover of the duel, since, in fact, this is the first affair of the kind I have ever been engaged in, and it is precisely for this reason that I wish to make one at this game."

"It is very fine for you to tell us this, my dear fellow: you not only play a game wherein your stake is life, but you leave to us, in the face of your family and friends, the responsibility of whatever may be the event."

"Oh, as to that, make yourself perfectly easy. I know my mother and my brother well ; when they ask you, 'Did Louis act as a brave and honourable man!' and when you shall answer, 'He did,' they will respond, 'It is well.'"

"But, deuce take it! we must know, after all, what weapon you would prefer."

"Well, well! if the pistol is proposed, accept it immediately."

"That's my advice, too," said the Baron.

"We shall take the pistol, then," said I; "since you both think it best to do so. But I think the pistol a murderous weapon."

"Is there time to learn to use the sword betwixt this time and to-morrow."

"No. In the meanwhile, you can take a good lesson from Grisier, that might possibly stand you in good stead."

Louis smiled. "Believe me," said he, "whatever may happen to me to-morrow morning is written above ; and all that you or I could do would not alter it one tittle."

We now shook hands and left him, to present ourselves at the residences of M. de Chateau-Renaud's seconds. Proceeding to the nearest, we found ourselves at M. Réné de Chateaugrand's, who dwelt, as we have said, at No. 12, Rue de la Paix. The gentleman was not at home to any one except parties coming from M. Louis de Franchi. We explained that we were there on the part of that gentleman, and giving our cards, were introduced immediately. We found M. de Chateaugrand to be perfectly unexceptionable as a man of the world. He would not listen for one moment to our taking the trouble to go to M. de Boissy's house, telling us it was quite unnecessary: and sent his servant to inform M. Adrien de Boissy that we were awaiting him. We amused ourselves in the interim by talking of hunting, coursing, racing, the opera—in fact, of anything excepting the business which brought us there. After ten minutes of this miscellaneous conversation, M. de Boissy made his appearance. Those gentlemen would not think of making any claim to choice of weapon: the sword or pistol were equally familiar to M. de Chateau-Renaud, and he would give M. de Franchi the choice or leave it to a toss-up. Throwing a louis into the air—heads for the sword, pile for the pistol—the piece fell pile upwards. It was then settled that the combat should take place at nine o'clock in the morning, in the forest of Vincennes; that the antagonists should be placed at twenty paces distant from each other ; that we should clap our hands thrice—at the third they should fire. We then left, to carry our answer to M. de Franchi. That same night I found, on re-entering my house, that Messieurs Chateaugrand and Boissy had left their cards.

CHAPTER XVI.

At eight o'clock in the evening I went to M. de Franchi's house, to ask him if he had not some instructions and commissions to give me: he begged me to wait until the morning, and in a somewhat strange manner, added, "I will consult my pillow."

Instead, therefore, of going to see him at eight o'clock in the morning, as I had intended, and which would have given us plenty of time to reach the rendezvous at nine, I was at his house at seven o'clock. He was in his library writing. He turned round at the noise I made on entering: and I saw he was very pale.

"Excuse me," said he: "I am writing to my mother: sit down, take one of the papers—I believe they have arrived: see, the *Presse* for instance: it has a very good *feuilleton*, by M. Méry."

I took the paper, and sat down, wondering within myself at the contrast which was exhibited by the livid pallor of the young man's countenance and the calm, grave, and soft tones of his voice. I tried to read, but though my eyes mechanically followed the words, the words themselves failed to present any idea to my mind.

"I have finished ;" said he, after the lapse of about five minutes ; and so saying, he rang the bell for his servant.

"Joseph, I am at home to nobody, not even to Giordano. Go into the saloon. I desire, without being interrupted by any one, to have five minutes' private conversation with this gentleman."

We were alone.

"My dear Alexandre," said he, "Giordano is a Corsican, his ideas are Corsican; I could not confide to him that which I have to entrust to you; he will keep my secret and that is all; but for yourself it is necessary that you should promise me to execute my wishes to the letter."

"Most assuredly I will : is it not my duty to do so, as your second."

"A duty the more important, as by so doing you will spare my family a second pang."

"A second pang?" asked I, in astonishment.

"Look !" said he ; "you see this is addressed to my mother—read it."

I took the letter from his hands, and I read as follows :

"My Good Mother,

"If I was not aware that you unite in your soul the heroism of a Spartan with the resignation of a Christian, I should employ every possible means in my power to prepare you for this dreadful stroke of affliction. Ere you shall have received this letter you will have only one son living.

"Lucien, my excellent brother, love my mother for both of us.

"Yesterday I was attacked by brain-fever; I paid but little attention to the primary symptoms: medical aid arrived, but too late ; my dear, good mother, I am given over—there is no hope for me, except by a miracle ; and what right have I to hope that God will exercise a miracle in my favour ?

"I write this to you in a lucid interval ; if I die, this letter will be posted within a quarter of an hour after my death, for, in the strength of my love for you, I wished that you should know of my decease, and that I die without regretting anything in the whole world except your love and that of my brother.

"'Look! said he; 'you see this is addressed to my mother—read it.'"—*Page* 44.

"Farewell, mother!

"Weep not for me, it is the soul that loves and not the body, and when I am gone my spirit shall conserve its love for you.

"Farewell, brother!

"Never quit your mother; think that now she has but you.

> "Your son,
> "Your brother,
>
> "LOUIS DE FRANCHI."

Having read the letter, I gave it back to him·

"What is the meaning of this?" I asked.

"Can you not understand it?" asked he, in return.

"No."

"I shall be a dead man at ten minutes past nine."

"A dead man!"

"Yes."

"Nonsense: this is folly.   What should strike you with such an idea?"

"I am neither silly nor idea-struck, my dear friend—in fact I have been forwarned."

"Forwarned! and by whom?"

"Did not my brother inform you," asked Louis, with a smile, "that the males of our family possess a peculiar privilege?"

"It is true: he did so," replied I, with an uncontrollable sensation of chilly dread, "he certainly spoke of an apparition."

"Louis took out his watch. 'I have now seven minutes to live!' said he."—*Page* 47.

"That is it. Very well, my father appeared to me last night: that will account for my excessive pallor—the sight of the dead has paled the living."

I looked at him with a vague and mixed feeling of terror and astonishment. "You mean to tell me you saw your father last night?"

"Yes."

"And he spoke to you?"

"He told me of my death."

"It is some horrid dream," said I.

"It is a terrible reality."

"Were you asleep?"

"I was awake. Do you not believe that a father can visit his son after death?"

I bowed in the affirmative, for in my heart I believed it possible.

"Tell me the particulars?" asked I.

"Ah, my God! the manner of its appearance was simple and natural. I was reading in bed—in fact, awaiting the appearance of my father, for I knew, if the thing was to end in death, he would appear, when at midnight my lamp suddenly became of itself low and almost extinguished, the door was slowly opened, and my father appeared."

"But how?" said I.

"Just as he appeared whilst living, and clothed in the dress he usually wore; but very pale, and his eyes fixed."

"God!"

"Then he slowly approached the bed: I raised myself on my elbow: 'Father, you are welcome,' said I. He came near me, and looked at me fixedly—and it seemed to me that his staring gaze was for a moment turned to a look of paternal love."

"Go on—this is indeed awful."

"Then his lips moved, and, strange to say, though his words were voiceless, I could hear them in my own heart, distinct and vibrating like an echo."

"What said he ?"

"'My son, think of God!' 'I shall fall then in this duel?' asked I. I saw two tears slowly roll from the fixed and glassy eyes down the pale and spectral cheeks. 'At what hour?' asked I; he turned his hand slowly and pointed to the time-piece: the hands stood at ten minutes past nine. 'All is well, my father,' answered I: 'the will of God must be done. I shall leave my mother, it is true, but I go to rejoin you.'

"A ghastly smile played on his bloodless lips, and, making me a sign of adieu, he retired: the door opened spontaneously at his approach, and shut in the same manner after his departure."

This narrative was told so simply and truly, that it was evident to me that either the scene had actually taken place, or that he was, by reason of the anxiety of mind, the victim of an illusion strong enough to have for him all the appearances of reality, and consequently its effects would be equally terrible.

I wiped the perspiration which poured from my brow.

"Now," continued Louis, "you know my brother!"

"Yes."

"You have an idea of what would be his conduct if he were to learn that I had lost my life in a duel."

"He would leave Sullacaro, immediately, to meet the man who had killed his brother."

"Exactly, and if he should be also killed, my poor mother would be thrice widowed—widowed by her husband—widowed by her two sons."

"I understand: it would be a frightful bereavement."

"Well: that is what I wish of all things to avoid. Then if they believe that I died from brain-fever, my brother will take no measures of revenge against any one, and my mother will be consoled more easily if she believed my death arose from a natural cause than if she knew I had been struck down by the hand of man. At least"—

"At least what?" interrupted I.

"Oh, no!" said Louis, "I hope that will not be."

I saw that he referred to a personal matter, and I desisted from pressing the question.

At this moment the door was opened.

"My dear Franchi," said the Baron de Giordano, "I have respected your injunctions to be private as long as it was possible. It is now eight o'clock—the meeting is fixed for nine—we have a league and a half to travel: we ought by this time to be on the road."

"I am ready, my dear friend," said Louis. "I have told M. Dumas all that I wish him to do."

Looking at me, he put his finger to his mouth. "As for you, my friend," he added, taking from the table a sealed letter, and handing it to me, "this is for you. If anything happens to me,

read this note, and comply, I pray you, with the requests contained in it."

"To the letter," I replied.

"You took care to have weapons ready?"

"Yes," I replied, "but as I was about to come here, I discovered that the cock of one of my pistols was somewhat out of order. We shall get a case of pistols on our road, at Devisme's."

Louis smiled as he gave me a look which fully indicated that he was aware of my repugnance to see him shot with one of my pistols.

"Have you brought a voiture, or shall I send Joseph to engage one?" asked Louis.

"I have my chariot at the door, and with a little squeezing it will hold the three of us; besides, as we are a little behindhand, we shall go somewhat quicker with my horses than you would if you hired a fiacre."

"Let us be off," said Louis. We found Joseph at the door.

"Shall I go with you, sir?" asked he of Louis.

"No, Joseph," answered Louis; "no, it would be useless—I shall not want you." Then, stopping a little behind, he added, "Here, my friend," and he put a little rouleau of gold in his hand, "if, sometime or other, in my moments of ill humour, I have been a little rough in manners or speech, I beg your pardon."

"Oh, sir," said Joseph, the tears starting to his eyes, "what does this mean?"

"Chut!" said Louis: and jumping into the vehicle, he placed himself betwixt us.

"He has been a good servant," said Louis, casting a last look behind him, "and if either of you can do him a good turn, I should feel grateful."

"Are you not coming back?" asked the Baron.

"No:" said Louis, smiling. "I have left him altogether."

We stopped at Devisme's just the necessary time to procure a pistol case, balls, and powder: and then went on at full trot towards our rendezvous.

––––––––

CHAPTER XVII.

WE reached Vincennes at five minutes before nine: almost at the same moment another voiture arrived, from the opposite side of the wood, at the same spot; it contained M. de Chateau-Renaud and his seconds. Five minutes after our arrival found us assembled at the spot agreed on.

"Gentlemen," said Louis, on leaving the vehicle, "you will understand, an arrangement of this affair is impossible."

"But," said I, approaching him—

"Oh, my dear friend, after the confidence I have reposed in you, you at least will understand that no person has the right to propose or receive any advances towards an adjustment."

I bowed before this will absolute—which, in fact, for me was supreme. Leaving then Louis standing near the carriage, we went towards M. de Boissy and M. de Chateaugrand. We bowed to each other.

"Gentlemen," said the Baron Giordano, who carried the case of pistols in his hand, "in circumstances like these the least ceremony is the better plan, for from one moment to the other we are not safe from the chance of disturbance. We were charged to bring the weapons—here they are; do you wish to examine them? They have been brought immediately from the gunmaker's, and we give you our words of honour that M. Louis de Franchi has never seen them."

"All this is quite unnecessary," replied M. de Chateaugrand; "we know we have an affair with men of honour." And taking one of the pistols in his hand, whilst M. de Boissy took the other, the two seconds proceeded to examine the weapons.

"These are pistols of the regular calibre, and have never been used," said the Baron. "Now, shall we load with one or two balls?"

"My opinion is," said M. de Boissy, "that each party shall load as it suits him, or according to his usual habits."

"Be it so," said the Baron Giordano: "we agree to everything that gives equal chances."

Whilst the other preliminaries of the duel were being gone through, and the pistols loaded, I joined Louis, who received me with a smile. "You will not forget anything of that which I have requested of you, and you will obtain a promise from Giordano—and which, by-the-bye, I have demanded of him in the letter I have given him—that he shall not inform my mother or brother of this affair. You will prevent also, if possible, the journals from publishing it: if inserted at all, take care that the names of the principals shall not be given."

"You are then still impressed with the horrid presentiment, that this duel will be fatal?" I asked.

"I am more than ever convinced of it. But you will do me this justice, will you not, that I met death like a true Corsican?"

"Your calmness, my dear de Franchi, is so great that it gives me a hope you are not convinced."

Louis took out his watch. "I have now seven minutes to live," said he; "here, you see this watch, keep it, I beg of you, as a remembrance of me. It is an excellent Breguet."

I took the watch, and shook him by the hand. "In eight minutes," said I, "I hope to return it to you."

"Don't speak a word more on that subject. See, here are the gentlemen coming to us."

"Gentlemen," said the Viscount de Chateaugrand, "there should be, a little to the right of this, a glade, in which, last year, I did a little business of this sort on my own account—shall it be there? It will be far better than to settle matters close to the path, where we should be liable to interruption."

"Lead the way, monsieur," said Giordano, "we will follow."

The Viscount took the lead, and we followed him in two groups. After thirty or forty paces of an almost imperceptible descent from the path, we found ourselves in the centre of a glade which at some distant period had formed the bed of a lake, but which, the water being drained off, was now a dry bog, surrounded on all sides by a sort of *talus* or sloping edge. The spot indeed seemed admirably suited to serve as a theatre for scenes such as was now about to be enacted.

"Monsieur de Martelli," said the Viscount, "will you measure the ground with me."

The Baron responded by a token of assent, and whilst this was doing M. de Franchi and myself were again alone.

"*A propos!*" said he to me, "you will find my will upon the writing-table I was using when you came in this morning."

"Very good," replied I: "make yourself easy."

"Gentlemen, whenever you are ready," said the Viscount Chateaugrand.

"I am here," said Louis. "Adieu, my dear friend, thanks for all the trouble I have caused you, without speaking," added he, with a melancholy smile, "of that which is yet to come."

I took his hand: it was cold, but evinced no trace of agitation.

"See you," said I to him, "forget this apparition of the night, and regard it as an omen of good."

"You recollect *Freischutz*."

"Yes."

"Very well, you know then every bullet has its billet. Adieu."

Meeting the Count Giordano, Louis took from him the pistol, without even glancing at it, and immediately took up his position at a spot indicated by a handkerchief. M. de Chateau-Renaud had already taken his place. For an instant there was a dead silence, during which the two young men saluted the seconds and their adversaries. M. de Chateau-Renaud appeared perfectly at ease and well up to those sort of affairs, and he smiled like a man sure of his skill; perhaps the knowledge that it was the first time that Louis de Franchi had ever had a pistol in his hand contributed somewhat to it. Louis was calm and cold: his fine head and pale face seemed like a noble antique bust.

"Gentlemen," said Chateau-Renaud, "we are waiting on you."

Louis threw me a last glance: then with a smile he raised his eyes to heaven.

"Now, gentlemen," said Chateaugrand, "prepare yourselves." Then striking his hands together, he cried out: "Once—twice—three times."

The two pistols were fired simultaneously, sounding like one explosion only. At the same moment I saw Louis de Franchi turn twice round and fall upon one knee. M. de Chateau-Renaud stood still, the ball had only gone through his frock coat.

I ran to M. de Franchi. "You are wounded," I said to him. He tried to respond, but in vain, a bloody foam appeared on his lips; at the same time he let the pistol fall to the ground, and raised his hand to his right side. I saw there was a hole, about the size of the tip of one's little finger, in his coat. "M. le Baron," cried I, "run to the barracks, and bring the regimental surgeon."

M. de Franchi signed to Giordano that it was useless, and made an effort to collect his energies. He then fell on both knees.

M. de Chateau-Renaud had disappeared, but his seconds came to the dying man's side. By this time we had opened his coat and torn aside his vest and linen, and we saw that the ball, entering his body below the sixth rib, on the right, had made its exit just above the left hip.

"I drew forth the watch; it was ten minutes past nine."—*I age* 48.

With every breath he drew, the blood came in jets from his wound. It was evident to all that the wound was mortal.

"M. de Franchi," said the Viscount de Chateaugrand, "we are very much grieved, believe us, at the result of this unhappy affair, and we trust that you have no enmity against M. de Chateau-Renaud."

"Yes, yes," murmured the wounded man, "I forgive him, but tell him to fly—to fly."

Then turning himself to where I stood, he said to me, "Keep your promise."

"Oh! I swear before God that I will do everything you desire."

"Now," said he, "look at the watch." So saying, and with a heavy sigh, he fell prone to the earth. That sigh was his last. I drew forth the watch; it was ten minutes past nine. I looked again at Louis—he was dead.

We brought the corpse to the house; and while the Baron de Giordano went to make the declaration before the Commissary of Police, I went up with Joseph, who cried like a child, into de Franchi's chamber. Casting my eyes on the mantel-piece, I was struck with the fact that the dial pointed to the exact time of ten minutes past nine. Doubtless he had forgotten to wind it up, and strange to say, it had stopped at that moment. Soon after, the Baron came back with the officers of justice, who put their seals on all the property in it. The Baron wished to send news immediately to the deceased's friends, but I

"When I opened my eyes, I found myself on the earth, in the arms of Orlandini, who was throwing water on my face."—*Page* 51.

begged him, before doing so, to read the letter which had been put into his hands by Louis de Franchi. This letter contained a wish that the knowledge of the cause of his death should be hidden from his brother Lucien, and also begged that as there were no intimate friends of his in Paris, that the funeral should be as private and quiet as possible. The Baron took all these affairs on his own hands; and I went immediately to seek M. de Boissy and M. de Chateaugrand, in order to beg them to keep silence on this unhappy occurrence, and to entreat them to use their joint endeavours to induce M. de Chateau-Renaud to leave Paris, at least for a short time. They promised to do all in their power to forward the wishes of the deceased; and I left them in order to post the letter which announced that M. Louis de Franchi was dying from an attack of brain fever.

CHAPTER XVIII.

CONTRARY to the general run of events, the duel made very little noise; even the newspapers, those braying trumpets of rumour and scandal, were silent on the subject. A few intimate friends followed the corpse of de Franchi to Père la Chaise.

Notwithstanding the pressing solicitations

made to M. de Chateau-Renaud, he had refused to quit Paris.

For an instant I had conceived the idea of following up the letter sent by Louis to his friends by one from myself; but though the end sought to be obtained was doubtless good, I had an invincible repugnance to write a falsehood respecting the dead to the young man's parent and brother: I was fully convinced also that Louis himself had hesitated in doing so. I had then, even at the risk of being accused of indifference or even of ingratitude, kept silence, and I was assured that the Baron had done the same.

I was sitting at the table, which I had drawn to the fire, about midnight of the fifth day after the event above recorded, and in no very pleasant mood, when my servant entered the room, shut the door quickly behind him, and in an agitated voice informed me that M. de Franchi wished to speak to me. I turned round and looked him full in the face; he was very pale. "Who did you say, Victor?" asked I.

"Oh, sir," replied he, "really—I don't know"—

"What! M. de Franchi is it that you say wishes to speak with me?"

"Monsieur's friend—him that I have seen here once or twice."

"You are dreaming, my dear fellow. Don't you know that we had the misfortune to lose him five days since?"

"Yes, sir, and that's the reason you see me so frightened. He knocked at the door, I was in the ante-chamber and opened the door; I started back immediately I saw who it was. He came in, and asked if you were at home. I was too much frightened to say more than 'Yes;' then he said, 'Go inform him that M. de Franchi asks to see him,' upon which I came to you."

"What nonsense! the ante-chamber was badly lighted, and you have been deceived: perhaps you were half asleep and did not hear perfectly. Go back, and ask the name a second time."

"It would be entirely useless. I swear to you, sir, that I have not been deceived at all; I have seen clearly and heard distinctly."

"Well—let him come in."

Victor turned half trembling towards the door, opened it, but took care to remain inside, while he requested the visitor to walk in.

I will confess that my first feeling was one of undoubted fear, as I lifted my eyes and saw in reality M. de Franchi before my eyes.

"Pardon me," said M. de Franchi, "if I have interrupted you by my visit at an unseasonable hour, but I have only arrived in Paris ten minutes since, and you can imagine that I did not wish to let the night pass without an interview with you."

"Oh, my dear Lucien!" cried I, running to him and embracing him, "is it you—is it indeed you?" And in spite of myself, tears escaped my eyes.

"Yes," said he, "it is I."

I ran over in my mind the time elapsed since posting the letter, and I found that it could scarcely have arrived at Ajaccio, much less Sullacaro.

"My God!" exclaimed I, "then you know nothing of what has occurred?"

"I know all," said he.

"How—all?"

"Yes."

"Victor," said I, turning towards my valet, who seemed as yet hardly recovered from his fright, "leave us, and come back in a quarter of an hour with supper. You will sup and sleep here, Lucien, of course?"

"I shall do both. I have not tasted food since leaving Auxerre. Besides, as no person knows me—or rather," he added, with a sickly smile, "everybody seems to take me for my poor brother, I do not wish to go out to-night, and leave your house in a state of consternation."

"The fact is, my dear Lucien, your resemblance to poor Louis is so great, that I myself was sensibly struck by it."

"How!" cried Victor, who had not yet left the room, "this gentleman is then the brother of"—

"Yes—but go you and serve supper."

Being now alone, I took Lucien by the hand and led him to a chair, and sat down by his side.

"But," said I, more and more at a loss to account for his knowledge of past events, "you were on your road when you received the fatal news?"

"No: I was at Sullacaro."

"Impossible: your brother's letter could not reach there before to-day."

"You have forgotten the ballad of Burger, my dear Alexandre, 'the dead are quick in their movements.'"

I shuddered. "What are you telling me? pray explain yourself, for I cannot understand you."

"Have you forgotten that which I told you of the ghostly appearances to our family?"

"Have you seen your brother?" I demanded.

"Yes."

"At what time?"

"During the night of the sixteenth and seventeenth instant."

"And what did he tell you?"

"All."

"He told you that he had died?"

"He told me he had been killed—the dead never lie."

"Did he tell you how?"

"In a duel."

"By whom?"

"By M. de Chateau-Renaud."

"No—no: I won't have that—no—no," said I; "you learnt that part of the intelligence in some other way."

"Do you believe I am in a mood for joking?"

"Pray pardon me: but, in good truth, that which you tell me is so very strange: in fact, all that has occurred both to yourself and to your brother, is so far beyond the bounds of the laws of nature"—

"That you cannot bring yourself to believe it —that's what you mean—is it not? I perfectly understand you. But look here," said he, opening his vest and linen, and shewing me a dark blue mark deeply impressed on the skin below the sixth rib on the right side, do you believe that?"

"Truly," I exclaimed, "in that part of his body your brother received his death-wound."

"And the ball came out here, did it not?" continued Lucien, putting his finger to a spot just above his left hip.

"It is indeed wonderful!" I exclaimed.

"And now—shall I tell you at what hour he died?"

"Say."

"Ten minutes past nine?"

"Stop, Lucien: give me the whole narrative in an entire shape. I lose myself amid my own questions and your fantastic answers—I should much better like to hear it in detail."

CHAPTER XIX.

Lucien leant back on his chair, and looking at me intently, continued:—

"Ah, *mon Dieu!* it is very easy to do that. The morning of the day on which my brother was killed I left home on horseback, with the intention of visiting our shepherds on the coast of Carboni: I took my watch from my pocket, looked at the time, and was about to put it back, when I felt struck by a violent blow on my side: I fainted. When I opened my eyes, I found myself on the earth, in the arms of Orlandini, who was throwing water on my face. My horse stood by my side.

"'What has happened?' he said to me.

"'Oh, my God!—I do not myself know. But have you not heard a gun fired?'

"'No.'

"'It appears to me that I have been shot in the side,' said I, shewing him the place where I felt the pain.

"'In the first place,' he answered, 'there has been neither gun nor pistol fired, and next, your clothes are not penetrated.'

"'Then,' said I, 'it is my brother who is shot.'

"'Ah,' replied he, 'that's another affair.'

"I opened my vest, and found this mark, as you see here—only there is this difference—that at the time I first saw it, it was red as blood.

"At first I was tempted, enervated as I was, both with anguish of mind and bodily pain, to return to Sullacaro: but then I reflected that my mother, who did not expect to see me until supper-time, would ask for the reason of my quick return; I could give no reason: and, on the other hand, I did not wish, without further corroboration, to announce my brother's death. So I kept on the road, and came home about six o'clock. My mother received me in her usual manner; it was evident she had no suspicion of evil. Supper ended, I retired to my chamber, but, in passing through the corridor, the wind blew out my candle; I was about to descend to re-light it, when I saw light shining through the chinks of my brother's room-door. Thinking that Griffo had been occupied in the room, and had probably forgotten to bring away his light, I pushed the door open; a wax taper stood near my brother's bed, and upon the bed lay his naked and ensanguined corpse. For an instant I was immoveable—paralysed by terror: the next, I approached the bed—I touched him —he was cold. He had received a ball through his body at the same part as I had felt the blow, and some sluggish drops of blood fell from the livid lips of the wound. It was then evident to me that my brother had been killed. I fell on my knees, and pressing my head against the bed, I shut my eyes and prayed to God. When I opened my eyes, I found myself in profound darkness, the taper was extinguished, the vision had disappeared. I felt the bed; it was empty. Listen! I must confess to you that although I am as brave as most men, yet, whilst I groped my way out of that room, I felt my hair stand on end, and the cold sweat of terror run down my brow. I descended the stairs to relight my candle; my mother met me, and cried out:

"'What has happened to you—what has turned you so pale?'

"'There is nothing the matter,' I replied; and taking another light, I again went up-stairs. I went into my brother's room; it was empty—the wax taper had disappeared completely, there was not the slightest impression of anybody having lain on the bed, on the ground lay the candle which had been blown out by the wind. Notwithstanding the absence of these or any new proofs, I had seen enough to convince me of the fact that at ten minutes after nine o'clock my brother had ceased to exist. I went to my own chamber, much agitated; as you may readily suppose, I was a long time before I could sleep, but finally fatigue mastered my anxiety, and I slept. In my sleep everything passed before my mind as a dream—I saw the whole scene as it occurred—I saw my brother's antagonist, the man who killed him: I heard his name pronounced—it was M. de Chateau-Renaud."

"Alas! all this is but too true," I replied, "but why have you come to Paris?"

"I have come to kill the man who killed my brother."

"To kill him?"

"Oh! rest yourself satisfied, I shall not kill him *à la Corse*, from behind a hedge or a wall. Oh, no: I shall kill him in the most approved Parisian fashion, in yellow gloves, frilled shirt, and ruffles."

"Is Madame de Franchi aware of your having come to Paris with this intention?"

"Yes."

"And it is with her permission you are here?"

"She kissed my brow and said to me 'Go.' My mother is a true Corsican woman."

"And you came?"

"You see me here."

"But whilst living, your brother distinctly wished the affair not to be avenged."

"Well, well," said Lucien, with a bitter smile, "he has changed his mind since death."

The valet now entered with supper; Lucien partook of it like a man free from all anxiety or pre-occupation; and I conducted him to his chamber, when we shook hands and parted. His manner had that calmness which, in men of strong minds, immediately follows the taking an unshakeable and determinate resolution.

On the morning after, he came into my room as soon as I was visible, and said to me, "Will you accompany me as far as Vincennes, I have a sacred duty that I must fulfil; if you are otherwise engaged, I will go alone,"

"How can you go alone—who is to point out the place to you?"

"I fell on my knees, and pressing my head against the bed, I shut my eyes, and prayed to God."—*Page* 51.

"Oh! I know it perfectly well. Have I not told you I saw it in my dream?"

I had somewhat of a curiosity to ascertain if he was possessed of this remarkable intuitive knowledge.

"Very well; I shall accompany you."

"Good: get yourself ready, then, whilst I write a note to Giordano: you will allow me to send your valet with it?"

"He is at your service."

"Thanks."

This affair concluded, we hired a cabriolet, and set out on our road to Vincennes. On our reaching the cross-road, he exclaimed, "We are very near it, are we not?"

"Yes," said I, "at twenty paces from here we shall be at the spot where we entered the wood."

"That's the place," said the young man, stopping the cabriolet as he spoke.

He had stopped at the very spot.

Lucien entered the wood without the least hesitation and as if he had well known the locality. He walked straight to the little glade, and when there, stood still a moment, as if to collect his thoughts; then, stooping towards the ground, where the sod was discoloured with a dusky red, he said, in a low voice, "This is the place;" and bowing his head slowly to the ground, placed his lips to the blood-stained herbage. Then, with flashing eyes, he stood upright, and looked around the little tree-bound glade for the spot from whence M. de Chateau-Renaud had fired.

"Here is the spot!" said he, striking the

"He touched me on the temple, adding, 'I shall put the ball just there.'"

ground with his foot; "here shall he himself be stretched lifeless ere to-morrow's noon."

"How!" said I, "to-morrow?"

"Yes, if he is not a coward, to-morrow morning he will give me a meeting here."

"But, my dear Lucien," said I to him, "it is not the custom in France to drag a man into a second duel because he has been the victor in a previous one. M. de Chateau-Renaud fought with your brother, because there had been a provocation. But that has nothing to do with yourself."

"Ah! truly: M. de Chateau-Renaud had a right to provoke and challenge my brother, because my brother offered his arm to a lady whom Chateau-Renaud had basely, cowardly deceived; and, according to what you say, he had a right to insult my brother. M. de Chateau-Renaud killed my brother, who had never touched a pistol in his life—M. de Chateau-Renaud killed him with as much security and certainty as I could kill that buck that is gazing at us—and I, his brother, I have not the right to insult M. de Chateau-Renaud? Let us go now."

I bowed, without answering him.

"Besides," added he, "you shall have nothing to do with the affair. Make yourself easy, then: I have written this morning to Giordano, and by the time we reach Paris, everything will be arranged. Do you imagine that M. de Chateau-Renaud will refuse my proposition?"

"M. de Chateau-Renand has unfortunately a

reputation for courage which, I confess, would not allow of the slightest doubt on such a point."

"Then everything is for the best. Let us on to luncheon."

So saying, we regained the road, and seated ourselves in the cabriolet.

"Driver," said I, "Rue de Rivoli."

"No, no : it is I who must be the host this time. Driver, to the Café de Paris. Is not that the house at which Louis usually dined ?"

"I believe it is," I replied.

"It is there, at all events, I have appointed to meet Giordano."

In an hour afterwards, we drove up to the door of the *restaurant*.

CHAPTER XX.

LUCIEN's entry into the saloon was a new proof of the strange resemblance betwixt him and Louis. The news of the death of Louis had gradually oozed out ; and though certainly not known in all its details, still it was common talk, and the appearance of Lucien in the Café seemed to strike every one with astonishment. I asked for a box, being aware that Giordano would join us ; and they gave us a little room at the end of the saloon. Lucien amused himself by reading the papers of the day with a *sang froid* which savoured almost of insensibility. Whilst engaged in discussing breakfast, Giordano entered. Though the two young men had not seen each other for four or five years, a shake of the hand was the only demonstration of friendship on their meeting.

"Well," said the Baron, "it's all settled."

"M. de Chateau-Renaud accepts the challenge, then ?"

"Yes ; but on one condition only : that he shall not be molested after this occasion."

"Oh ! he may rest assured of that ; I am the last of the de Franchis. Is this communication from himself or his seconds ?"

"From himself. He has engaged to inform Messieurs de Boissy and de Chateaugrand. As regards the fixing the hour and the place, and the choice of weapons, all that is left to ourselves."

"All right. Now sit down to breakfast."

The Baron took a seat, and the conversation was turned into other channels. After breakfast Lucien asked us to take him to the commissary of police who had sealed Louis's effects ; and also to the proprietor of the house in which his brother had resided. He wished to pass the last night before the consummation of his vengeance in Louis's chamber. All these affairs took up the greater portion of the day, so that it was nearly five o'clock before Lucien entered his brother's apartment. We there left him : the sanctity of grief should ever be respected. Lucien had before named the time of meeting for eight o'clock on the next morning ; and he begged me at the same time to procure the pistols used on the former occasion, and, if possible, to purchase them for him. Starting for Devisme's shop, I concluded a bargain with him for the pistols for 600 francs. The next morning at a quarter before eight, I was at Lucien's

abode. I found him, on entering, in the same seat, and writing on the same table, and in every respect in the same position, as I had on a recent occasion seen his brother. There was a smile on his lips : but a pallor on his face.

"Good morning," said he. "I am writing to my mother."

"I trust that you will send news less distressing than that which eight days since was sent by your brother."

"I have told her she can now pray tranquilly for her son, for that his death was avenged."

"How could you speak with such certainty ?"

"My brother foretold his own death to you : I foretell to you that of M. de Chateau-Renaud ;" and rising as he finished speaking, he touched me on the temple, adding, "I shall put the ball just there."

"And for yourself ?"

"He will not touch me."

"But, surely, you could at least wait the issue of the duel before sending your letter."

"That would be perfectly useless ;" so saying he rang the bell. "Joseph," said he to the valet, "put this letter into the post."

"You have," said I, "then seen your father."

"Yes," was his reply.

It was a strange circumstance, the occurrence of those two duels, one following the other, and in each case the death of one of the parties being known beforehand. However, in the interim, Giordano had arrived, and as it was now eight o'clock, we set out. Lucien was in such haste to reach the place of meeting, that his exhortations to the driver to push on had the effect of bringing us to the spot full ten minutes before the time appointed. Our antagonists reached the ground at the exact time : they were on horseback, with a mounted domestic in attendance. M. de Chateau-Renaud carried one hand in his bosom ; in fact, I thought at first sight that he carried his arm in a sling. Dismounting at a short distance, they threw their bridles to the domestic, and approached, as M. de Chateau-Renaud remained somewhat in the back-ground ; but distant as we were from him, I could see him turn very pale as he threw a glance at Lucien. However, he turned round directly, and, with the riding whip he held in his hand, amused himself by decapitating the little wild flowers which reared their heads above the green verdure.

"We are here, in obedience to your challenge, gentlemen," said M. de Chateaugrand ; "but you of course know the conditions on which we alone accept it, that is, that this shall be the last duel, whatever may be its results. M. de Chateau-Renaud will not answer to any person for a double event."

"Perfectly right," responded Giordano on our part, to which Lucien added a sign of his assent.

"You have the weapons, I believe ?" asked the Viscount de Chateaugrand.

"We have."

"And they are unknown to M. de Franchi ?"

"Much more so than to M. de Chateau-Renaud, for he has used one of them very lately, whilst M. de Franchi has never yet seen them."

"Very good ; come, Chateau-Renaud."

We immediately plunged into the wood without even uttering a single word more, each one occupied with a painful recollection of the scene of which this had so recently been the theatre, and feeling a presentiment that something not less terrible was about to be re-enacted. On arriving at the little thicket-bound glade, M. de Chateau-Renaud, by dint of extraordinary nerve, appeared calm, but those who had seen him on the former occasion could appreciate the difference in his manner at the present moment. From time to time he cast a furtive glance at Lucien, and this look betrayed an uneasiness which narrowly resembled that of fear. Perhaps it might have been that in the strange resemblance of his present antagonist to his former victim, he believed that he saw in Lucien his brother's avenging shade. Whilst the pistols were being loaded I saw him take his hand from the breast of his coat; it was enveloped in a wet handkerchief, with a view to restrain feverish agitation. Lucien looked on with a calm and fixed eye, as if he was assured of his revenge; and, without waiting for any one to place him, he took his position on the exact spot of ground on which his brother had last placed his feet; this, as a matter of course, obliged M. de Chateau-Renaud to take up the position he had before occupied. Lucien received his weapon with a joyous smile; M. de Chateau-Renaud, on taking his pistol, pale as he was before, now turned actually livid, then he passed his hand betwixt his neck-tie and his throat, as if his cravat was suffocating him by its tightness. No idea could be given to the reader of the feeling of involuntary awe with which I looked at this young man—full of health and good looks, blessed with all that could make life pleasant—rich and fashionable—waking each morning full of hope and joy, and with an expectation of many years of life—to-day, standing with the cold damp sweat on his brow, and the deep throes of anguish at his heart, conscious of his being the next moment stretched on the earth a corpse.

"Are you ready, gentlemen?" asked M. de Chateaugrand.

"Yes," answered Lucien.

M. de Chateau-Renaud made a sign of assent.

As I did not dare to look at this scene, I turned away my head. I heard the two clappings of the hands, the third was immediately followed by the firing of the two pistols. I turned round, M. de Chateau-Renaud was stretched at full length on the grass, stark dead, killed without heaving a sigh—without the movement of a limb. I approached the dead man, spurred by that irrepressible curiosity which forces us to see the finale of a catastrophe; the ball had entered at the temple, at the precise spot which Lucien had indicated to me. I ran up to the latter he stood calm and motionless, but on seeing me approach within arm's length, he threw himself into my arms.

"Oh! my brother! my poor brother!" cried he, as he burst into a fit of sobbing. They were the first tears the young man had ever shed.

THE END.

W. S. JOHNSON, "NASSAU STEAM PRESS," 60, ST. MARTIN'S LANE, CHARING CROSS.

"He threw himself into my arms. 'Oh, my brother! my poor brother!' cried he, as he burst into a fit of sobbing. They were the first tears the young man had ever shed."—*Page* 55.

www.ingramcontent.com/pod-product-compliance
Lightning Source LLC
Chambersburg PA
CBHW081215170626
46811CB00010B/3300